GUNSLINGER REVENGE

MOONLIGHT MESA
ASSOCIATES

OTHER TITLES BY
JERE D. JAMES

The Jake Silver Adventures:

Gunslinger Justice - Book VI
Back from the Dead - Book V
High Country Killers - Book IV
Canyon of Death - Book III
Apache - Book II
Saving Tom Black - Book I

GUNSLINGER REVENGE

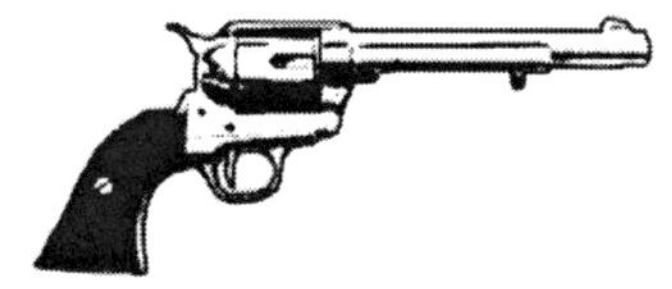

Jere D. James

GUNSLINGER REVENGE

PRINTED IN THE UNITED STATES OF AMERICA

Published by

Moonlight Mesa Associates, Inc.
Wickenburg, AZ

www.moonlightmesaassociates.com
orders@moonlightmesaassociates.com

ISBN: 978-1-938628-26-9

LCCN: 2015913389

Cover painting by Vin Libassi

1

"Hold still, you little wench!" Floyd Baker clamped his filthy hand over the young girl's face and stuffed a well-soiled handkerchief in her mouth. Her attempts to escape greatly humored him, and he enjoyed her futile attempts to break free. For a little thing she fought like a bobcat. "You're a pretty little gal," he drawled. "And I like a woman with some spirit. You'll do just fine."

"We ain't got time for this nonsense, Floyd," Jarvis McKinney hissed. "Let that girl alone. I don't want no posse comin' down on me for kidnapping a little girl."

"Well, you just go on your way then," Floyd snarled in response, a hateful look in his eye. "I'll keep your share of the money, too, if you're goin' to get all sissified and righteous on me."

Holding the flailing girl as easily as if she were a kitten, Floyd Baker squared up to Jarvis McKinney, his height and heavy, muscular build daunting. Even more intimidating, however, was Baker's face – unforgettable in its ugliness. The big man's pock-marked, whiskered, and knife-scarred visage alone was frightening, but what scared folks the most were the man's eyes that seemed to aim in different directions. Baker's nose, flattened a few times too many, and his rotted, black teeth completed the terrifying picture of a monster.

Jarvis hesitated and squirmed nervously while he watched Baker upend the girl and laugh as she shrieked in fear.

Baker carried the struggling bundle to his horse and mounted. Once seated, he smacked the girl's face, which took the fight out of her long enough for him to settle himself and gather the reins. "Now, let's you and me take a little ride up to the woods," he whispered. Once again the girl began to twist and writhe as tears flowed down her cheeks.

"Don't you go ruin this for me by bawlin'," Baker commanded. "I'll have to hurt you real bad if you start that whinin' and cryin'." He watched her eyes and chuckled at the fear in them. Then he spurred the horse to a lope up the long, dirt road toward the pass leading to Crown King. Jarvis McKinney reluctantly followed.

An hour later, Baker dumped the girl on the ground and quickly dismounted. Stunned by the fall, it took the captive several moments to gather her wits. Before she could stand and run, however, Floyd Baker fell on her, his weight crushing her into the ground.

"Now, I like to know my gals. What's yer name, sweetheart? Don't make me ask you again," he said, drawing a knife from his belt and flashing it next to her face. "You wouldn't want me to leave my mark on you now, would you? So, just tell me your name. Whisper it real soft like in my ear, honey."

"Floyd, I think you done scared the girl enough," Jarvis offered.

"Josephine," the girl finally managed to choke out in a quivering voice. "Please let me go, mister. My pa will pay you money if you'll let me go. I promise he will."

Floyd laughed. "Well, Josephine, I'll go see your daddy right after we finish our business here. But I got a real, strong hankerin' right now, and nothin' ain't gonna stop me from relievin' that urge."

Floyd momentarily paused, distracted by the girl's beauty. Not nearly as robust as he liked, she looked exquisite with her creamy complexion, long auburn hair and large hazel eyes. Although she was a sight to feast on, he had other things on his mind.

Floyd jerked the girl's dress up and roughly spread her legs with his own. He took the knife and sliced away at her garments. "Saves time doin' it this way, don't ya think? Drives me wild watchin' women strippin' down. Can't control myself. This way, I still got my pleasure comin'," he whispered, leaning over her drooling and rubbing his coarse beard on her delicate face.

The click of a revolver stopped Baker, who slowly turned his head toward Jarvis. "What in Sam Hill do you think you're goin' to do with that gun?"

"I'm gonna have to shoot you, Floyd, if you hurt that girl," Jarvis replied. "I won't tolerate it, I won't. You got no right to hurt that little gal. She ain't part of our plan."

Quickly Baker stood and turned toward Jarvis. "You done plain lost your mind, Jarvis. You pull a gun on me, you best be prepared to kill me, cause I sure as hell gonna kill you if you don't."

"Don't want no bad feelings between us, Floyd. We been ridin' together for a good spell, but I won't stand for that girl to be abused. Plenty of whores around who will pleasure you. You leave that girl alone. She's barely out of childhood. And I'm meanin' what I say." Jarvis boldly stood his ground as he cocked the hammer on a second revolver.

Floyd studied his partner for a moment, then turned to Josephine. "Normally, I would get to know you better, sweetheart, but not right now. You're about the pertiest gal I've ever had, though, so I'm gonna take you with me. If you're smart, you'll keep your mouth shut, or I'll cut your tongue out," he said. "I got me a collection of tongues in my saddlebag. Wanna see them?"

Josephine shook her head and curled into a little ball on the ground, whimpering.

"I'm gonna make us a nice little camp here, Floyd," Jarvis said after a few tense moments. "This is a good spot. Quiet and isolated. We can divide up the money we took from that store and then plan what we're gonna do next. We'll send that girl on home at daylight."

Floyd snorted in disgust, but he nodded.

While McKinney set about gathering a small stack of wood, Floyd kept his eyes on Josephine. He wanted to take her along with him. She was a beauty, but he knew that she would attract attention. People would question why a beautiful little girl was riding with an ugly lout like him. A pity to kill the girl, but maybe it would be for the best. Still, he could have his way with her if he killed Jarvis. The idea tempted him mightily, but he hesitated. Despite his fury at Jarvis' comeuppance, Floyd had to admit the man was the master at crafting plans and coming up with new ideas.

"I gotta thank you, Josephine. You been a real pleasure to gaze on, darlin'. Don't think I can turn you loose in the mornin', though, like my partner wants. You seen and heard too much, gal," Floyd said, out of earshot from Jarvis.

Josephine squeezed her eyes closed and did not move.

"We'll have us some fun before I take off in the mornin'," Floyd said. "Hey, you want a little whiskey? Might make you feel a bit better. Loosen you up some."

After taking a long swig from a bottle he pulled from his pack, Floyd offered the drink to Josephine. She shook her head which aggravated him. "You bein' rude, you little snot." He studied the girl for a moment, then shrugged his shoulders and took another long swig. "More for me, I guess. Jarvis here, he don't drink. He don't take to women like I do either. That man don't know half of what he's missin'."

He tossed a piece of jerky to the girl, who again shook her head. "I'm not hungry," she whispered.

"You need to keep your strength up for me, darlin'."

Another sob escaped the girl. "I hate you," she finally said. "I hope you die."

"Well, you are a little hell cat. I gotta give you some credit, girl. You just makin' me right proud of you."

Josephine gritted her teeth every time Floyd leered at her. If the man called Jarvis couldn't control the one named Floyd, she knew she'd be killed after he had his way with her. He'd have no choice but to kill her. Her pa and brother and half the men in Waggoner would ride the man down, torture him and hang him. She would laugh and spit on him when he begged for mercy...if she was still alive. Just picturing his capture and torment distracted her from his terrifying appearance and verbal assaults. *I have to escape, or he'll kill me!*

She sensed that sweet-talking Baker would never work, but it might work with the man named Jarvis. Besides, she refused to lower herself by obliging Baker in any way. Obviously she couldn't overpower the two of them, unless she got hold of a gun. Now, that was a possibility, but only if both of them took off their gun belts before they slept, which she doubted would happen. Josephine feared Baker might even kill her before he slept. She stared into the small fire while he continued with his filthy talk. She could burn him up if she could reach a limb.

At 15-years of age, Josephine was very capable. Raised on a small ranch, she worked beside her pa almost every day after she finished her studies. She hated the studies, but it was her mother's one demand if she insisted on working with livestock and in the fields like a common laborer. No school work, no farm work.

I have to gather my wits if I want to survive and escape, she thought. Her mind remained a blank, however, despite her struggle to think. When the brutish man finally sat to roll a cigarette, she tried to smile but it came out more of a grimace. "What's your name?" she asked in a small voice.

She watched him study her for a moment. "Floyd. And I think you know damn well what it is since you heard ol' Jarvis here call me by that name."

"Floyd, you've made quite an impression," she said, fighting back the venom and hate she felt. She involuntarily shuddered as she watched the man lick his lips and leer at her.

Floyd smiled. "My pleasure, Josephine. We'll consort in the morning when Jarvis heads up to Crown King. Man needs to rest up, you know. I've had a long, tough day. Killin' always leaves me a bit tired. Now some men feel full of energy after killin' someone. Not me."

Again Josephine tried to smile but failed. Instead she nodded as she watched Floyd take another drink. Would he get drunk on that amount? Hope began to surge as she imagined him snoring in drunkenness while she crept away.

"Gonna tie you up there, Josephine, so's you don't get any ideas about sneakin' off in the middle of the night," Floyd said as he moved toward her. Kneeling down, he ran his hands over her body, grinning evilly as he roughly bound and hog tied her. "Now, little gal, I'm done tuckered out, so I'm gonna take a little snooze. Jarvis here, he'll probably try to read to you from the Good Book." Floyd guffawed as he walked away. "How that man can spout the Bible and murder folks at the same time baffles me." With that, he emptied the bottle and settled back against his saddle. Within minutes Josephine heard his heavy breathing along with an occasional snort.

Jarvis returned after a bit and laid out his blanket and then stoked the fire. "I won't let this ne're-do-well do you no harm, miss." Almost instantly upon settling back and closing his eyes, Jarvis too began to snore.

Quietly squirming and wriggling toward the fire, Josephine rolled to her side and carefully backed up to the small campfire and grabbed for a thin limb laying alongside the low-burning flames. Craning her neck to watch, she cautiously she pulled the red-hot stick away from the embers and tried to place the smoldering wood against the rope connecting her bound hands and feet. She moved carefully lest she set her clothes on fire. After a few moments she could smell the rope slowly melting. The heat from the limb quickly died out, so she scooted even closer to the fire and pulled another burning stick from the small pile of limbs. A second thin limb did the trick, although it also singed her dress and burned her hand.

She laid still for a spell and watched her attackers sleep and drool. Then, after studying the fire for a few moments, she once again scooched back toward it and pulled another stick from the mass. Carefully withdrawing the burning stick, she twisted her wrists about and, despite the pain, she held the smoldering end of the small branch against the rope securing her hands. Awkwardly twisting her neck to see, she tried to keep the glowing end away from her clothing. The hot end of the stick slowly licked away at the wrist binding enough for her to break the bonds and pull her hands apart.

Hands freed, Josephine remained perfectly still and watched her adversaries for what seemed an eternity, her heart pounding. Convinced they both slept soundly, she slowly sat upright, untied her ankles and stood. Although tempted to run pell-mell through the woods, she forced herself to cautiously back away from the slumbering men, keeping an eye on them and on the ground lest she step on twigs or brush against bushes that might arouse the deadly sleepers. Momentarily she thought of taking one of their horses, but she feared the commotion would awaken the men. Would she be fast enough to escape her evil captor if he awoke to find her trying to mount one of the animals? She didn't think so.

Once out of sight of the campfire, Josephine turned about and waited a moment for her eyes to adjust to the inky dark. Still having no night vision, however, she could not stop herself from moving forward. Although she moved as stealthily as possible in the pitch black, the noise she made sounded to her like loud trumpetings and crashes.

Several hours later Josephine stumbled onto the dirt road leading to Waggoner. Although slower, she decided to walk ten feet to the side of the road in case the horrible man awakened and stalked her. She didn't fear Jarvis, but Floyd Baker scared her near witless. Despite resolving to remain calm, she soon began running through the trees and brush, tripping, falling, and whimpering. What seemed a long while later, she espied a moving light in the distance. She knew it would be her father searching for her. "Papa?" the girl whispered. "I'm here, Papa. Please find me!"

Josephine lurched to the road and ran as fast as she could. As the distant light slowly drew closer, she detected the faint sound of familiar voices. "I'm here," she tried to yell, her dry throat making her voice barely audible. "Help me! Please! Please! Papa! I'm here!"

Floyd Baker heard Josephine's cries for help as he trotted down the road. He'd awakened to find the girl missing and had erupted in fury. In the distance he could just make out the shape of the girl running down the lane. "Foolish little bitch," he cursed. "I gotcha now." He moved the horse into a lope. A light appeared to move toward him, but it didn't deter him. Furious, he only wanted to punish the girl for escaping. He fumed at her audacity. Never had any woman defied him, and she would not live to brag about it.

As he drew closer, he heard her feeble cries, and his mouth contorted into a smile-like sneer in anticipation of victory. The light had advanced steadily toward him, but suddenly it stopped moving. Floyd pulled his weapon from its holster and fired at the lantern. Almost immediately it was extinguished and an answering shot rang out causing him to slow his pace.

A rising moon lit the Waggoner valley like a gas lamp, and Floyd spurred the horse to a faster pace. He made out a small group of riders ahead, and he began firing at them. He watched the group scatter at the sound. Enraged that he would most likely not be able to track them all down and grab the girl, he emptied his gun at the fleeing riders and then pulled his rifle from its scabbard intending to use it. Cursing loudly, he abruptly reined his horse around and raced back toward the safety of the wooded mountain, irate that he'd been foiled by a simple girl and a handful of stupid, damn sod-busters. Had he known a lucky shot had found Billy Williams, Josephine's young sweetheart, he'd have felt much better.

2.

"Richard Moody, what prison train did you ride into town on?" Jake Silver asked, warmly clasping Moody's hand.

There – fleeting but unmistakable, Moody saw sadness pool briefly in the Marshal's grey eyes.

Moody smiled at the man before him. "Good to see you again, Jake." He paused, not certain what to say. He wondered if he should express his condolences about Betsy, but it felt awkward somehow. Maybe later.

Richard felt Jake scrutinizing him. "Let me buy you a beer. Or coffee since you're looking so official with that new badge and promotion and all," Moody finally said.

"Sure. I'll meet you at Sooty's. Just down a ways on the right. Let me finish up one thing here," Jake said. "Five minutes."

Moody stood on the boardwalk and surveyed the busy street. He'd heard through various sources that Jake had been offered the promotion to U.S. Marshal when he'd returned to Prescott after Betsy's murder. Obviously, her death had undone all his well-thought-out plans of retiring from law enforcement and resuming ranching.

Strolling down the street, Richard couldn't help but notice the change in Prescott. It had always been a booming little town, but now it seemed much more like a city – maybe still a tad small compared to eastern cities, but probably not for much longer.

Sooty's was only half filled, so Richard looked about for a table that was private, yet would also give Jake a chance to keep an eye on everything – if he still had that annoying habit.

"Coffee for two," Moody said to the waitress. "And you got any pie?"

"Yes, sir. We have apple, peach, and rhubarb. You want cream with that coffee?"

"I'll take an apple and a peach. No cream."

Richard tried to relax. He knew he had to acknowledge Jake's loss, but damned if he could think of how to broach the subject. He felt like hell for not contacting him much sooner. Three years was too long to wait to express condolences. He slowly stirred his coffee, wondering why he hadn't been more of a friend. Jake Silver was the only man he could trust, the only man who knew him and his reputation and didn't try to kill him for the reward.

"You look deep in thought there, Richard," Jake said, smiling and pulling out a chair.

"I was. Listen, Jake, I…I want to tell you that I'm real sorry about Betsy. I should've contacted you. For some reason I just couldn't. It all seemed so…so…."

"Unbelievable?" Jake finished the sentence. "I know. There wasn't much you could do, Richard. Don't fret about it."

"I don't feel good about my absence. I'm sorry, Jake. Regardless, I should've been there."

"Listen, the two kids kept me plenty busy, plus I came back here to Prescott. Couldn't stay in that big fancy house Betsy had built over in San Diego. I needed help and I figured Virginia Hall would be the best person for that given that both kids knew her well. I got offered the promotion to the Marshal's job as soon as I got back. Couldn't turn it down. Wanted to, but what the hell would I do all day without Betsy around? Plus, I didn't want to spend down my daughter's inheritance –

which is substantial – but still, I had to get busy doing something or I'd have gone crazy."

"You living in the log house here that Betsy bought?"

"Yeah. Technically it belongs to our daughter Maggie, so that's good. And I had Betsy buried on the property by her sister and former ranch hand Thomas Jefferson Sr. It's home for the kids – and for me, at least for now."

"I gotta ask, Jake, I'm sorry, but do you know who did it?"

"All the evidence points to Ben McGraw. In my gut I know it was him. He no doubt wanted revenge for Gunner's death. He never believed, like no one else did either, that you pulled the trigger and shot Gunner. Everyone knows Betsy shot and killed Gunner after that little bastard back-shot me."

"You're quite certain it wasn't the big Mexican?"

Jake shook his head. "No. He would kill me. Not Betsy. It wouldn't have been his way at all."

"McGraw still alive and walking around? That's hard to believe."

"I'm not in a situation to pursue him right now, Richard. One you'll find hard to understand."

"Try me."

"Richard, I have two kids now. My daughter and Margaret's boy. Betsy would rise from her grave and kill me if I didn't take care of Maggie. Trust me, McGraw's day will come, and revenge will never be so sweet. But I don't want my daughter to be an orphan."

"Well, Jake, the problem with revenge, you know, is you need to dig two graves. 'Before you embark on a journey of revenge, dig two graves.' That's courtesy of Confucius by the way, not Shakespeare."

Jake smiled sadly and nodded. "That'll be okay – when the time comes."

Both men turned to the slices of pie that had been set before them and ate in comfortable silence. After the last bites had been scraped from the plates and the coffee refilled, Jake asked, "What brings you to Prescott, Richard?"

Richard mulled around the best answer to give. "Let's just say I've worn out my welcome everywhere else in the country."

Jake nodded. "So I've heard."

"Things haven't gone real well for me since we went our separate ways. The old way of life is a tough one to make a living at what with all the damn people flooding west. Can't go out and kill a bad man anymore without onlookers and the law's long arm hounding you."

"Well, you have to admit you were always a bit brazen in executing your prey."

"Maybe," Richard replied with a small laugh. "But still, a man's gotta make a living. How many warrants are out on me?"

"I haven't seen one for a couple of months, to be honest. But I don't look too closely," Jake said, winking conspiratorially. "So, what's your plan? You just passing through or aiming to stay for a spell?"

"Not sure. My main goal was to see you and try to make amends for not, you know, showing up or…anything. I'm very regretful about that."

"Tell you what," Jake said, leaning across the table closer to Moody. "I might have some work for you. Why don't you come out to the house this evening. Have some dinner. See the kids. We'll talk then. More privacy. Plan on spending the night."

Before Moody could answer, Jake stood and walked away.

"Well, I'll be damned. He stuck me with the bill again," Moody muttered, a smile visiting his face.

Carrying around two weeks of travel residue, Richard spent the afternoon getting a shave, bath, and haircut. He had his clothes cleaned as much as possible while at the bath house. He spent the rest of the afternoon in various saloons eavesdropping where possible, hoping to pick up scuttlebutt about any possible work.

He left for the ranch shortly after 3:00, remembering that it took a bit of time to ride out there, unless one chose the hellish shortcut which he felt quite certain Jake probably rode if he came into town every day.

The trip to the ranch brought back myriad memories, some not so good, others downright pleasing. Lost in his recollections, Moody was surprised when the large log house appeared against a wooded hillside, lush pastures surrounding three sides of the structure. The drive leading to the house wound through towering pines. A quiet pervaded the property, broken suddenly by the growing sound of excited snorts, whinnies, and thundering hooves. A small herd of horses raced to inspect the new animal walking up their drive and then followed along, high strung and skittish. Moody's own mount began to respond accordingly, and finally he had to circle the animal a few times to calm the edgy critter.

As he approached the corral by the barn, Moody was pleased to see Thomas Jefferson, Jr. emerge from the shadows, the man Betsy had hired to be her ranch hand in San Diego. Jefferson's father had also worked for Betsy when she first arrived in Prescott.[1]

"Howdy Mr. Moody. I suspected you was coming along."

"Still predicting the future are you, Mr. Jefferson?"

"Nah, sir. I only felt you nearby. Didn't predict nothing," Jefferson said, a big smile on his face.

"Is Jake here yet?"

"Yes, sir. He rode in about an hour ago. Told me to send you up to the house when you arrived, and for you to leave your horse with me for the night. I'll tend to him, sir."

---

[1] *Saving Tom Black, Book I*

"Mighty kind of you, Thomas," Moody said, dismounting and handing the man his reins. "You come over from San Diego with Jake?"

"Yes, sir. Mr. Jake was in a mighty bad way there for a spell. We all was. Miz Hall, she come over and got the children, and then Mr. Jake and me come over a bit later."

"I'm glad you're here, Thomas."

"Well, Mr. Jake done right good by me. He give me all the horses that Miz Betsy was raising and breeding and a place to live. I do my best to keep this place in tip-top shape. He even helped me fix up my father's old room down here. Made it much bigger," Thomas said as he led Richard's horse into the large barn and began unsaddling him. "I don't need much on account of Miz Hall does all the cookin' and things like that. She a mighty busy woman, but she seem real happy. She's gettin' on up there in years, though. Not sure how much longer she gonna want to work the way she does."

Thomas Jefferson's soft voice and slow, easy manner made Richard feel more relaxed than he had in weeks. He remembered all the heckling he'd given Thomas about being able to foretell the future and had to smile at the memory. The man had eerie abilities, there was no doubt. He wondered if Jefferson had foreseen Betsy's murder. He'd ask him at a more appropriate time.

"I know you is wondering about Miz Betsy dyin' and me not forewarning her," Thomas said as he brushed the horse.

"No, not at all," Moody lied.

"Now see here, Mr. Moody, I can't stop bad things from happening. I sensed something real evil, and I warned Miz Betsy not to let nobody come around until Mr. Jake got home. I didn't know for certain who the evil person was, or if there really was one. I've been wrong a few times and I didn't want to scare her none." Thomas led the horse back to the corral and turned the animal loose. Moody followed along, unable to resist the man's almost hypnotic speech. "I just knowed something wasn't right. I knowed it back when we was on that big ship returning to San Diego." Both men watched as the horse dropped and rolled in the fine, powdery dirt. "I never felt so bad in all my years as when that bullet pierced that pretty girl's head. I wanted to die myself right then and there. T'wasn't right. Just t'wasn't right. Then, I figured the next best thing I could do was devote my life to seein' that Jake and his little girl was cared for. I do my best, sir. Do my best."

Mesmerized by Thomas Jefferson's long speech, Moody finally said, "I'm sure you do, Thomas. Jake is lucky to have you."

Moody wanted to ask if there was anything Jefferson might foretell about his own future, but resisted.

"Now, I know you are plenty curious about your future. So, I can tell you that I don't see no evil hurtin' you yet."

"Would you tell me if you did?" Richard asked.

Thomas Jefferson paused a moment. "No, sir. I most probably would not. But I will say that I see you goin' on a long trip. Now, you go on up to the house. I be joinin' you soon."

Richard walked up the drive to the house, his mind occupied with Thomas Jefferson's revelations.

3.

Never comfortable around children, Richard Moody paled under the scrutiny of eight-year-old Maggie Silver. To begin with, he'd been caught off guard when he'd entered the house and found the girl cleaning a rifle on the dining room table.

"You needn't stare, Mister. I know what I'm doing. I've been taught by the best," she said archly.

"Yes, I'm quite certain you have," Moody replied, unable to muster a better answer.

"My father is in his office. He's expecting you. Do you know the way?" she asked, looking at him fully.

The girl was the image of her mother. Blonde hair, azure-colored eyes, beautiful face, and an impudent, coquettish manner. Moody stood, shifting his weight from foot to foot, completely nonplussed.

"You are Richard Moody, I presume?" the girl asked, standing and wiping her hands on a cloth.

"Yes. I'm Richard Moody."

"I'm glad you've come, actually," Maggie continued, taking Moody by the hand and leading him deeper into the house. "My father seems very happy this afternoon. You must be a good friend of his. I'll look forward to getting to know you – perhaps." With that she ushered him into Jake's small office. "He's here, papa. Your friend is here."

Jake looked up and smiled. "Thank you, Maggie. Have you introduced yourself?"

"Not exactly. I didn't feel the need. I'm certain he knows who I am, since he's your friend." She smiled at Richard. "Just in case you don't know me, my name is Maggie Silver. My cousin out there is Henry. He picked that name himself after he saw my mother's Henry rifle on the wall. He didn't like his other name." With that the girl curtsied and left.

Jake chuckled as Richard, momentarily speechless, stared after the child. "You've got your hands full, Jake. She's quite precocious to say the least," he finally managed to say.

"Smart as whip – maybe too smart – but don't mind my bragging." Jake stood and moved toward a cabinet housing several bottles of alcohol. "Care for a drink?"

"That's a good idea."

The two talked aimlessly until Virginia Hall announced that dinner was ready. It was a meal Richard wasn't particularly eager to attend since he knew that Virginia had never approved of him or his friendship with Jake. However, enough chatter ensued at the table that he never had to make polite conversation with the woman.

Besides Henry and Maggie, Thomas Jefferson also dined with the family. Talk included ranch issues, school work, and lots of laughing. Moody saw that Jefferson had a natural, relaxed manner with the kids, occasionally reprimanding them in such a way that they didn't realize they'd been reprimanded. Jake didn't seem to mind in the least that a black man spoke thusly to his children, and Virginia Hall accepted Thomas' comments as though they were pearls of wisdom from above.

Despite the relaxed manner of everyone at the table, Moody still felt on edge, as though waiting for a reprimand from Jefferson or Virginia. Or worse yet, Maggie Silver.

After dinner the children mysteriously disappeared along with Thomas Jefferson who briefly assisted Virginia in the kitchen. The two men moved to the porch.

Neither spoke for several minutes, listening to the music of crickets and an occasional hooting of an owl. Now and then in the distance a horse nickered. Finally, Jake spoke. "Richard, if you're interested, I have a job that would suit you perfectly. Are you at all wanting to hear about it?"

Moody thought about Jake's comment for a few seconds only. "I have nothing else, Jake. What's your pleasure?"

"Well, I have a well-meaning, young Deputy U.S. Marshal, but the problem is he's still darn green. A lot of potential though. Lot of potential. The kid's a good shot. Handles a horse like he was sired by one. But he's young and green and knows no fear. That's the troubling part. I don't want to see the kid get killed. And he will if someone doesn't take him under their wing."

"I'm not much at being a wet nurse, Jake. And I don't think I'd be the best teacher."

"You'd be perfect at both," Jake replied, laughing. "Listen, this kid is smart. He learns fast. He'll be a great deputy given just a little time. Let him tag along. Besides, I've got some big assignments for you and an extra hand might be welcome."

Moody perched on the porch railing, looking out into the dark.

"Listen, Richard, I'd do these jobs and invite you to join me, but you see what I've got here. I can't abandon Maggie the way I kept doing with Betsy. Besides, my job now is technically a desk job, although I do get out and warm up the pistols a bit, but I can't be gone for extended periods."

"Yeah. I understand your predicament – I guess," Moody answered sullenly.

"I'm itching to go after Ben McGraw, Richard. I dream about it. But I'm not going to dessert my kid. Not after what we've been through."

"She remember the…incident?"

"Hell yes. I was surprised about that too. A few months after we returned here she started having godawful nightmares. She'd see Betsy's head with the hole in it. This went on for a year or longer. Finally, one day she announced at the table that she would kill the man who killed her mother. Virginia almost fainted. I assured her I'd take care of the man when the time was right. Still, she gets that look in her eye. You know what I'm talking about."

"Jake, I think maybe you're reading too much into it. I hope so, anyway."

"If you're around here long enough, you'll see it in her. She's got the nerve for it. She's asked for a rifle for Christmas for the last two years," Jake said, sighing.

"Yeah. I saw her cleaning a rifle when I came in."

"Listen, I'd like you to consider a job working for the U.S. Marshal's office. I'd like to have you back here in Prescott, at least until you get the itch to move on," Jake said.

"Where do I sign on the dotted line?" Moody asked. "I got nothin' to do, Jake, and nowhere to do it in. I always liked this town, anyway."

The two shook hands. "Come by the office tomorrow. I'll get you set up, swear you in and give you a fancy, tin badge," Jake said. "And, Richard, thanks. This means a lot to me." After a moment he continued, "Now, you want to use a room here in the house or sleep down in the barn's extra quarters?"

"You know, I think I'll like sleeping under the same roof as Thomas Jefferson rather than Virginia Hall." They laughed as they headed toward the barn. "That woman isn't any too fond of me. She makes me right fidgety."

"You'll get use to her. She's a damn good cook, and she takes great care of the kids."

"I been meaning to ask," Richard said as they walked along, "how's little Henry?"

"He's quiet. Thoughtful. Doesn't talk a lot, but always has something intelligent to say when he does speak. He's a good kid. Smart as a whip. Maggie's all energy and emotion. Henry is thoughtful and observant."

Moody nodded. He'd been surprised to see Henry, although he couldn't say why. He'd known the boy as a toddler when he'd been deeply in love with Margaret, Betsy's sister, back before everything had gone to hell.

"Whatever happened to your nephew?" Jake asked, remembering that Richard had gone looking for the boy after Richard's sister died.

Richard looked down and shook his head. "I never found him, Jake. I searched all over Illinois, Missouri, and Kansas. I went to every boarding school I could find in the mid-West. Not a trace of him. It's haunted me, I have to tell you. Really haunted me. Sometimes I feel like I didn't look long enough, or hard enough. I don't know."

"I'm sorry to hear that."

"I posted notices in newspapers – even hired a private detective. Me – hiring a detective! Nothing. I have to assume the kid died somehow. I don't know. Makes me sick to think or talk about it. Even my sister's death haunts me."

"It's a shame. All of it." Jake paused for a bit. "Seems like there was a time when the two of us were hell bent on being killed – the risks we took. I never pictured Betsy being the one who'd take a bullet in the head. Never imagined your sister ending up like she did. I guess I figured that Mexican outlaw would be the last of me."

"You ever hear from that man?"

"Only rumors that float across the border from time to time."

"What was his name again?"

"Diego Fuentes."

"That's right. Diego Fuentes." Richard walked in silence for a few moments. "That was some adventure, Jake. Can't believe either one of us lived through it."[2]

Jake nodded.

---

[2] *Back from the Dead, Book V*

They reached the barn and found Thomas Jefferson up, fussing with the horses. He nodded a greeting as the men entered.

"You going to leave any hide on those animals?" Jake asked.

Thomas smiled in response, then said, "I groomed your horse, too, Mr. Moody. He a bit slow-moving for you, ain't he?"

"That's the truth," Richard said. "He was the only gelding for sale. Paid too much on top of it."

"Tell you what, Mr. Moody, if you gonna be around for a time, I got a mighty nice horse that needs some ridin'. I be pleased if you was to take him for a spell. Got to warn you, though, he's young and not quite finished. Just needs some saddle time and miles on him," Thomas said, moving to a fresh-looking sorrel. "I call him General, 'cause he thinks he's boss. You can call him any cussed thing you like."

Moody looked the horse over. "Nice piece of horse flesh here, Thomas. You sure you want him ridden by a gunslinger? It's a dangerous occupation."

"Oh, you gonna be just fine, Mr. Moody. No worries there. Least not as far as I can see."

Richard felt almost a sense of relief hearing Thomas Jefferson's prediction. "Well, if you're sure about that, I'd be a fool to turn you down."

"Careful, Richard," Jake piped up, "you might be the fool to take him. Thomas Jefferson is clever at these negotiations."

"Naw. Now, Mr. Jake, you know better than that," Thomas laughed.

"Sure, I'd like to give him a try," Richard said.

"I'll shoe him for you first thing in the morning," Thomas said. "He be ready by, let's say, 9:00. Meanwhile, I made up the bed for you in my room. You sleep in there tonight. I know you got to be tired. I got work to do, so I'll just sleep in the stall here."

Richard turned pale as he remembered that one of the last nights he ever spent with Margaret was in the room Thomas now used, a room filled with too many memories. “No. I’ll stay up at the house, Thomas. You keep your room. I just came down to check on my horse.”

4.

A lanky, dark-haired, young man welcomed Moody with a, "Humph. So, you must be the infamous Richard Moody. Jake told me to expect you."

"Jake around?" Moody asked, not responding to the kid's disdainful greeting.

"He'll be back in a minute. Told me to tell you to take a seat. So, take a seat."

Moody turned to exit the room to avoid a confrontation with the rude kid, but Jake entered the office almost immediately. "Good. Glad you're here. Have you two introduced yourselves yet?"

"No mistaking who this guy is," the Deputy U.S. Marshal said. "His picture's plastered all over those posters you always destroy." Squaring off to Moody, he added, "I'm Daniel Cleary."

"*Christ! An Irishman!* What have you got against me, Jake?" Moody asked with mock anguish. "You expect me to be a wet nurse to an Irishman?" He smirked as he watched Cleary bristle at the comment.

"Well, I see you're both off to a good start," Jake said. "Things are going better than I expected."

"Hey! I may be Irish, but at least I'm no lowdown gunslinger."

"Not yet," Moody responded. "Listen, Jake, I think your idea here may not be the best. I better take a pass on your offer."

"Nonsense," Jake answered. "Danny here is just testing you. He wants to keep this job, so I know he'll be a willing student," Jake said, glowering at Cleary.

Cleary looked away and slowly nodded. "Yes, sir. Like the Marshal says," he said, turning to face Moody, "I will appreciate all the tips you can give me. But I don't take to being cursed as an Irishman."

"Well, at least you're not a red-headed, freckled one. The Black Irish may be the most troublesome, but they're the best of the bunch. You've got that going for you," Moody said.

"Okay, we got that settled," Jake commented. "Now let's do some serious talking."

Jake set about explaining the details of their expedition. "You're not going far, only to Crown King, but you may need to ride into Waggoner. Even still, it's not a bad two-day ride on well-packed, dirt roads. You ought to be able to find out what you want, or even find who you want, in a relatively short time. If you're still empty-handed after four days, come on back."

"I don't suppose there are hotels in this mining area?" Moody asked in a mocking, hopeful tone.

Cleary scoffed. "What's the matter, old man? Don't like sleeping out?"

Moody ignored the taunt. "Of course, I suppose there's bound to be a brothel. But you're too young for that," he said, glancing at Cleary.

"Sleep where you like," Jake said. "You're on your own. Turn in expenses when you return. But know the expenses get paid sooner if the job gets done."

"We leave today, or early tomorrow?" Moody asked.

Cleary snickered and started to make a retort about Moody being old, but one glance from Jake hushed him.

"Tomorrow will be fine. Get some supplies. There'll be food available in the mining camps most likely – for a price – so if you can't agree on supplies which you can charge at the mercantile, better take some money to pay for your grub." Jake paused and looked at both men. "Everything clear?"

"Tell me about the man we're looking for," Moody said.

"Make that men. Don't know much about them, Richard, only that they killed a man in the Waggoner area, beat up an old man and kidnapped a young girl. They were seen heading toward Crown King. There's myriad mining camps dotting the area. They could be miners, or they could just be drifters," Jake said, "roaming around the high country causing a lot of trouble. I've heard the name Floyd Baker bandied about. Not sure who the other one is."

Moody tensed and his usual poker-face betrayed him.

"You know Baker?" Jake asked.

Moody hesitated for a few moments, but his hesitation had answered Jake's query. "I knew a Floyd Baker back when I was a kid," he finally admitted. "Bad apple, that one. Probably not the same Floyd Baker, though."

"You okay with this job?"

Moody smiled, but only his lips moved. "Not a problem. I'm looking forward to it."

"I heard one of them killed a man over a girl," Daniel offered. "A cousin of sorts from down that way told me."

"That's certainly a solid, reliable source, I'm sure," Moody said.

"Damn right it is. My cousin works up there for one of the mining companies. Said two men rode in and one of them was wanting a woman, but none of the whores up there would have anything to do with him. They got thrown out of the only establishment in the area serving beer and they headed on down to Waggoner, thinking maybe to find a gal, but no such luck. Heard tell he tried to grab a young girl, or did grab her – no one's really saying for sure what happened or who got grabbed – but it ended in a gunfight and he killed the girl's father, or brother, or someone," Daniel reported, a supercilious look on his face.

"So, what you're saying is no one knows who got grabbed, or if they got grabbed, or who challenged the guy," Moody sighed. "That's sure a lot of helpful information there, Cleary."

"Okay. We're about finished here," Jake interrupted. "You two get your supplies and take off in the morning, or now. Suit yourselves. But Daniel, you're to go with Richard and *remain* with him. Have I made myself clear?" Jake asked.

Cleary nodded sullenly.

Jake looked questioningly at Moody, but the gunman avoided eye contact.

It didn't take long for the two riders to arrive at the immense mining region. Well-traveled roads crisscrossed the scarred, mountainous terrain. Because of large clear cut areas, mining settlements were easily spotted. The two men quickly discovered that many of the mining sites had been abandoned, however. Although a few people stayed on in hopes of a mine's revival, most moved on to the next promising site. The few remaining locals eyed the two strangers warily regardless of their badges, so Moody advised that they continue on and not stop, despite the youth's objections.

"People aren't going to talk when they don't trust you," Moody said, "unless you stick a gun in their faces. No point in broadcasting what we're here for. The smart ones will figure it out. Eventually someone will be brave enough to tell us what we want to know. You won't get any cooperation out of these people by threatening them. They could be scared of retaliation from the outlaws, among other things. They may not even know anything – maybe they haven't even see the men in question." Moody paused and studied the sullen faces as they rode by. "My guess is if they knew anything, they'd be eager to speak up. These people aren't. When we meet up with people who've had first-hand dealings with these men, they'll be anxious to talk."

"Your best guess?" Cleary scoffed. "How come you're so all fired knowledgeable if you've always been on the wrong side of the law?"

"It doesn't take a genius to figure some of this stuff out, kid. You need to pay closer attention to your boss. Jake Silver is, hands down, the best lawman I've ever encountered."

"He can't be that good if he lets the likes of you run around," Daniel retorted.

Moody cast a scornful glance at the boy.

"I don't get it. I figure you must have something on him. He gets drawers-full of wanted posters with your picture plastered all over them and just tosses them out. He never even posts them like he's supposed to. I figure pure and simple you got something on him."

"You figure, do you?" Moody smiled. "By the way, watch that snare up ahead. It'll cripple your horse if he steps in it."

"Where? I don't see no snare," Daniel replied skeptically, looking along the trail. Nevertheless he fell in behind Richard, who pointed the deadly trap out as they rode by.

"Do more observing and less jawing," Richard advised.

"Now who would plant traps like that?" Daniel asked.

"Just about any ne'er-do-well who wants your money. Indians set those too. They usually want your scalp, though, along with your weapons and horse…if it can still walk."

The two rode in silence for the better part of an hour before Cleary spoke. "So, how'd you meet Jake, anyway?"

"I was hired to kill him," Moody answered.

"You two known each other a long time, then?"

"A spell."

"You want to know how I met him?" Cleary asked. Moody offered no response, but Cleary continued anyway. "I actually didn't meet him 'til I came to Prescott. But I heard about him first from this real young kid that got hired on a ranch where I was cowboyin'." After taking a long drink from his canteen, Cleary continued. "Yeah. My boss hired this real young kid who showed up and gave a big sob story about how he was an orphan and all that. But the kid could ride and rope some, so my boss, Big Bill Barnes, put the boy in the bunkhouse with all us hired hands.

"Well, the weeks go on and the kid's a real talker. Pretty soon he starts talkin' about having lived up in some rim country in Arizona – he called it a rim, anyway – and how this marshal came ridin' in one day and what a great guy he was and how he saved him and his mom's lives. It sounded kind of made up, but it also had the ring of some truth in it. It sounded real exaggerated, though, you know?"

Moody quickly became very attentive. Cleary sounded like he was telling the story of Jake coming upon his sister Katie Reed and his nephew Buddy when they'd lived up on the Mogollon Rim in Arizona. "What was this kid's name?"

"Called himself Buddy. Never gave a last name that I recall."

"When did all this happen?"

"Well, let me think on that. Let's see," Cleary began. "I come to Prescott about a year ago. The marshal'd been there for a spell. So, I'm guessing I first met that kid about four years ago, maybe five. He was mighty young at the time. Maybe 10 or so. Can't rightly remember."

"What else did he tell you?" Moody asked after a bit, yawning and trying to sound only half interested.

"Not much. Most of it sounded like he made it up. But one night we was all in our bunks and the kid – he bunked next to me – he said that he sure missed his mom. I asked when she died, and he said she didn't die. He confessed that she'd sent him away to school so he wouldn't take to the cowboy life. He said he got off the train on one side while his mom stood on the other waitin' for the train to pull on out. Said he didn't want to go to some fancy school back East. He wanted to be a cowboy and ride horses all day."

"Hmm," Moody replied. "You're right, sounds pretty made up to me," he commented in an offhand manner.

"Well, I kinda thought so too, but the kid had real tears in his eyes. The next mornin' he announced that he was goin' back to San Diego to see his mom. He sneaked on out in the middle of the night about a week later, and I never seen him since. But I remembered the stories he told about Jake Silver, so when Jake's woman got killed, all the newspapers carried the story. One of them mentioned Silver – the 'famous lawman' they called him – was headin' back to Prescott. After a few months I decided I wanted to do something with my life besides rope cows, so I took off for Arizona. Hadn't planned on meetin' Jake. I just thought of goin' to Arizona 'cause that's where the papers said Jake was headin'. Thought it sounded like an interestin' place what with the kid's stories and all."

Moody asked, "Did he ever say, by chance, what his mother's name was or give other details?"

"Hmm. Don't recall right now. He might've. Why? You think you know her?"

"You never know," Moody answered. "So, you never heard from the kid again?"

"Nope. He just took off. Stole a gun from one of the guys. Leastwise we were all pretty sure the kid stole it. Took a horse too, but the boss said the horse wasn't worth much and to let the kid go. I think the boss took a likin' to the kid. Probably reminded him of his own son that died when he got gored by a bull. Hard to tell."

A mountain of thoughts and questions raced through Moody's head. Could the Buddy in Daniel Cleary's story actually be the nephew he'd spent three years looking for? Moody had searched all over the midwest for his nephew, but he'd not even considered looking elsewhere. He tried to silence his thoughts and save them for later. He could see a small settlement ahead and he needed to pay attention.

5.

A stream of tobacco juice briefly sizzled on the low-burning fire. A fierce scowl blanketed Floyd Baker's face. Everything had gotten all balled up when that girl got away from him. He watched Jarvis bring in an armload of small limbs. It was getting downright damn cold at night, but Jarvis insisted they keep the fire low in case someone was looking for them.

"Ain't nobody gonna come up here lookin' for us, McKinney," Baker whined. "Them country Bible-thumping folks is all in their warm houses probably sippin' coffee and stokin' up a big blaze in the fireplace."

"It's not worth the risk, Floyd. People don't take to men grabbin' young girls the way you done. Best to stay out of sight and get the hell out of these mountains."

"How we gonna rob any gold deliveries or high-grade any ore if we leave? Huh? You answer me that one," Baker said in a scornful voice. "The tailings we've gone through have been picked over. I bet we ain't got $50 worth of gold."

"We're not stayin', Floyd. We'll have the law all over us any day now. They're probably already combing these hills. We've stayed too long as it is."

"So, what's your plan, then? Or do you even got one?"

"What abouts we head on to Mexico for the winter?" Jarvis asked, looking up at his grizzled partner as he put a few small limbs on the sputtering fire.

"Mexico? I don't know nobody in Mexico. Why would I go there?"

"That's good. You see, if you don't know anyone, then it's likely no one knows you. So we'd be safe."

Jarvis could see Baker pondering the proposal.

"Not a half bad idea, I suppose," Baker said after a few minutes. "Say, how far is Mexico from here anyways?"

"Maybe a week's ride. Depends on how hard and fast you want to travel," Jarvis answered.

"I don't know. I gotta think on that."

"Well, don't spend too much time thinkin', 'cause I've already thought about it and that's where I'm headin'. You can go with me or stay here, but you're on your own if you stay," Jarvis said, standing and wiping dirty hands on his soiled pants. "I'll probably read about your hangin' in the paper when I get to Yuma."

Baker squirmed uncomfortably on the log he'd perched on and inadvertently ran his fingers between his neck and shirt. "Fine. Mexico suits me fine if that's what you're wantin'," he finally said, "only when we run outta money, don't look to me."

"We won't run outta money, Floyd. There's lots of opportunities to rob folks on our way south. We can live like kings in Mexico, and there's lots of young girls for you there, too," Jarvis added on the spur of the moment to make the trip irresistible. "Anyhow, I'm leavin' first light. I got a bad feelin' about this area. You wanna come with me, that's fine. Otherwise, we split what we have and go our own ways."

"Humph. Guess I'll go along with ya. Got nothin' else to do."

"We'll pick up some supplies in Yuma. Meanwhile, we're going to have to lift a few goods to get us through. I was countin' on the gold from the mines like you were, but that's not goin' to work for us now," Jarvis explained.

"How we gettin' out of this area without goin' through Waggoner?" Baker asked.

"Floyd, there's more than one road." Jarvis shook his head at his partner's stupidity. How he'd hooked up with such a simpleton was inexplicable. He'd half hoped that Baker would choose to go his own way; however, the man would come in handy when it came to robbin' folks or banks. Baker knew no fear, that was certain. And he was damn good with a gun. That counted for something – made up for some of his stupidity anyway.

Jarvis spread his saddle blanket on the ground close to the fire and pulled his coat snugly over his top half and under his chin. It would be a long night, and he hoped it would be the last night he'd have to spend in the area. He speculated about their upcoming journey for several hours, figuring if they left early in the morning and rode hard, they might be in Mojave by nightfall, or close, anyway. The Indians there wouldn't bother them if they stayed well away from their encampment. Then, they could follow the Colorado all the way down to Yuma. There wasn't much law in the area, but there would be a lot of miners and greenhorns searching for their motherlode. It would be easy pickings for two outlaws to take advantage of the solitary men roaming the desert. They could shoot every one of them and no one would be the wiser. The bodies would likely mummify beyond recognition in a short time if the vultures and coyotes didn't tear them apart first.

Jarvis' past travels had taught him that most of the miners carried a goodly amount of supplies, so it'd be easy living all the way south. And the greenhorns all wore those stupid money belts that broadcast to any man with half a brain what they were. He shook his head in amazement that so many men were so stupid. Now women seemed to be a lot more conniving and suspicious. He stayed away from women as a rule, unless it was a down and out soiled dove. And unlike Floyd, Jarvis didn't take to hurtin' little girls. "Shameful," he muttered. He'd probably have to kill Floyd before long. The man was trouble, that was certain, and he had unscrupulous ways and sinful habits.

He cast a glance at the snoring man on the other side of the fire pit. *Hell, I could kill him right now and probably save myself a lot of grief,* he thought. But he didn't. He didn't like the idea of being a back-shooter. Besides, he had a gut feeling that Floyd would come in handy.

As the fire's embers slowly faded, Jarvis dropped into an uneasy sleep. Several times he opened his eyes and stared into the darkness, certain he'd heard whispering and twigs snapping under the weight of humans. He swore he smelled smoke from a distant campfire. He stared into the darkness until his eyes felt they would bug out. Overhead, the passage of the stars was barely noticeable. Would morning never come?

"Some men, two of them, rode through here about four, five days ago. Well, maybe it was three days ago," Joshua Logan said. "We weren't none too hospitable. The men had a bad look, if you know what I mean."

"I do," Moody answered in a low voice. "Did you by any chance get a good look at them?"

"I looked as best as I dared. I didn't want to get shot for bein' too snoopy, you know. Some folks is mighty touchy about you lookin' at 'em, and I gotta say one of those men was so downright ugly it was hard not to stare," Logan said, his head bobbing vigorously.

"Ugly? How so?" Moody asked.

"Well, just…just ugly. Like he had a bad pockmarked face, and one eye was kind of strange to look at. The one eye, it looked in one direction and the other eye looked the opposite way. Gave me the chills, I gotta admit."

"Anything else?" Daniel Cleary asked.

"Well, his nose looked like it'd been broken maybe half dozen times. And when he grinned at my wife, I swear his teeth was all half-rotted. Gives me the willies just thinking about it."

"You've been very helpful," Moody said. "What about the other man?"

"Can't rightly say. I was so spooked by the ugly one I could hardly take my eyes off him," Logan continued. "I wanted to shoot the bastard for leering at my wife like she was a common whore, but…."

"You made a wise decision not to do that," Moody said. "If the man is who I think he is, he's a cold-blooded murderer. We'd be standing over your grave now had you drawn on him."

Logan nodded. "Still…."

"He may come back through here," Cleary offered. "He caused a ruckus down in Waggoner and got away, so it's possible he may still be roaming around this area."

"Yeah. I heard about him grabbin' a young girl. Hope he didn't do her no harm."

"Thanks for your help, Mr. Logan," Richard said as he turned his horse about. "If that man comes back, keep your distance."

Exasperated, Cleary wheeled his horse about. "We're not going to stay? They invited us to eat, Moody. I'd like a decent meal instead of tack and old stale biscuits and your bitter coffee."

"These people don't have enough food for themselves right now, Daniel. The mine has been closed for weeks. No work. No food. We'll travel until dusk then set up a camp."

Moody heard Daniel sigh heavily. "Fine."

Two hours later Moody reined his horse to a stop. "This looks as good as any place," he said, dismounting. "There's some water in that rain catchment.

Cleary looked around. "I suppose," he said, dismounting. "Why aren't we heading back to Prescott? Jake said to come on back if we couldn't find the culprits."

"We've got water and firewood. Can't ask for much more. Why don't you water the horses while I build the fire?" Moody suggested as he unsaddled, ignoring Cleary's question about returning to Prescott.

After a moment of hesitation, Cleary asked, "Any Indians around, you think?"

"I doubt it, but you best keep a good eye out. Most of them have pretty much left the area or been killed off. But there's always a chance that a renegade or two might still be around."

Because of the thickly treed area and the surrounding hills, it grew dark quickly. Once Cleary had eaten some stale biscuits soaked in hot coffee, his stomach stopped gnawing at him and he grew less sulky and more talkative.

"I remembered some more stuff about that kid I was telling you about," Cleary said.

Moody didn't respond, but Cleary took no notice.

"This kid used to talk about his uncle some, too. Seems the uncle was kind of an outlaw. Kid never said his name that I can recall."

"An outlaw? Like a bank robber?"

"No, he never really said. Just said the man was an outlaw type. That kid sure thought highly of that man, though. I was thinking maybe you might have known him, you being a friend of Jake Silver and Jake knowing this boy and his ma."

"I don't know," Moody replied. "Maybe I saw him. Hard to say." His curiosity piqued, Moody continued. "He say anything else about the uncle?"

"Kind of hard to remember, it's been so long ago. He probably did." Cleary paused for a few minutes. "You know, I think I remember the kid saying his uncle had a girlfriend that was Jake Silver's girlfriend's sister. That make sense? I don't know. The more I think about it the more I think the kid just liked to talk about Jake Silver."

No doubt, not that there'd been much earlier, remained in Moody's mind that the boy Cleary talked about was his sister's lost nephew.

"You have no idea what happened to this kid?" Moody asked after several minutes.

Cleary shrugged. "Probably ended up on the wrong side of the law like most runaways."

"You ever mention any of this to Jake?"

"Nah. Never thought about it."

"So what about you?" Moody asked. "How'd you come to be at that ranch?"

Cleary chuckled. "I was a runaway, but a bit older than Buddy when I took off. I guess some people would just say I took off and not think of it as running away. I was fifteen when I left home."

"You sound like you might be from Missouri," Moody said.

"Damn. You're good!" Cleary said. "You're right. I come from Missouri. Made my way west by hoppin' railcars and working here and there. Once saw a big shootout on a train in Texas even. I sneaked into a passenger car and was sitting there like I belonged, when these two men opened fire. Holy mackerel. Bullets were flying in all directions. People got shot. It turns out this marshal named Gosling, I think it was, was escorting two men to the penitentiary. I'm not sure who all was related to whom, but I'm telling you when shots started ringing out and women started screaming, I hid under the seat and said my prayers. I didn't want to be no witness at any trial, so I skedaddled damn fast the minute that train came to a stop."

Moody didn't respond to Cleary's account, so the two sat quietly for a bit.

"Hey, I been meaning to ask, who is the man that Mr. Logan was describing?" Cleary asked. "You said you knew who he was."

"Can't say for sure, but I'm thinking it's a no good, ignorant, murdering fool named Floyd Baker, a pathetic excuse of a human being if there ever was one."

"Tell me about him," Cleary said excitedly.

"I think I already said it all," Moody commented. "Do yourself a favor, though, if you ever run across the man, go the other direction. Unfortunately, he's damn good with a gun and has no qualms about shooting anyone – man, woman, or child."

"He faster than you?" Cleary asked. "Jake says you're about the fastest there is."

"He's fast. Faster? Hard to say."

"So how'd your paths cross?"

"You need to quit talking, Cleary," Moody said, turning his head as though listening intently to a distant sound.

"You hear something?"

After a few minutes Moody replied. "There's someone out there. I can feel it."

Cleary looked about uncertainly. "You feel it? That's supposed to convince me?"

"Keep your gun close and your mouth closed. No more wood on the fire. I'll keep the first watch while you get some sleep."

Moody kept watch much longer than his allotted time. He couldn't stop thinking about his missing nephew. He knew for a certainty the boy that Daniel talked about was Buddy, his dead sister's son. For the life of him, Moody couldn't understand why his sister, a wealthy woman after her husband's death, had taken up with Vincent Cooper and gone into the Superstition Mountains looking for the Dutchman's Lost Mine. Moody didn't believe the mine existed, yet every year the skeletal remains of gold seekers who'd gone in search of the hidden riches were found. Had the Apaches not taken Vincent Cooper and Katherine that might likely have been their fate. Instead, Katherine Reed's fate had been far worse.

Repeatedly raped, beaten and terrorized nightly by the Apaches, Katherine had given up all hope of rescue. Humiliated, and with a broken spirit, she'd plummeted too far into the depths of hell to recover. Cooper, meanwhile, had been rescued in his escape attempt.

Moody had seen to it, however, that Cooper paid the ultimate price for dragging his sister into the entire escapade. Jake Silver had been part of that retribution.

Although the rescuing soldiers had taken Katherine to Fort Apache where she'd been under a doctor's care, she died after several weeks and, unable or unwilling to speak, the whereabouts of her only living son remained unknown. Moody suspected she'd been too humiliated to live.[3]

Richard only knew that Katherine had sent the boy to school back east in an effort to keep him from becoming a "cowboy," a career the youth apparently found intriguing. But despite his extensive three-year search, he never found the boy. If Daniel was right, and Richard had no reason to doubt he was, Buddy had never even left California. So, where might the boy be now? Surely by now the kid would have discovered that his mother was gone.

Richard tried to ignore the urge to go in search of Buddy. *I'll do it after this job,* he told himself. After all, the kid had been on his own all this time anyway. Still, the memory of his sister dying, with a solitary tear rolling down her cheek, brought a surge of anger and guilt. It was the least he could do for her – he'd do it later.

---

[3] *Gunslinger Justice, Book VI*

6.

"Now where we off to?" Daniel asked after suffering through a morning of silence.

"Heading down to the Waggoner area," Moody replied. "I told you yesterday."

"Why the heck aren't we going back to Prescott like Jake told us to?" Daniel asked, clearly exasperated.

"Why? Because I don't give up on a job, that's why," Moody snapped. "Tell you what, kid, you can hightail it back to Prescott if you've a mind to. When I take on a job, I do the damn job and I don't let anything else get in my way," Moody said, scowling.

"Fine. I'll do that," Daniel replied, his face flushing in anger. "At least I know how to follow orders."

Neither spoke as they saddled up and gathered their belongings. Moody mounted and, without saying a word or looking back at Daniel, set off through the forested land heading toward Minnehaha Flats and Waggoner. Pausing a moment, Daniel cursed loudly then reined his horse about and followed a few lengths behind Moody.

After an hour Daniel shortened the gap between him and Richard, and before long he rode slightly to the right and behind him.

Getting no reaction from Moody, Cleary finally asked, "What're you going to do in Waggoner?"

"I'm going to have a chat with a few folks. It's called 'investigating.' That might be a new tactic for you to think about instead of repeating hearsay and gossip."

"Mind if I come along?"

"Only if you keep your mouth shut and don't embarrass yourself."

"You know, Moody, you're a hard person to like. I don't see what Jake Silver sees in you."

"Times were different when Jake and I were riding together," Moody said after a few minutes. "Neither of us had ever suffered a loss. We never worried about losing someone to a murdering varmint. Now we both have. It changes a person. Knocks the wind – and pride – out of a man."

"I heard you and Jake shot upwards of nine men up on the Mogollon Rim one time," Daniel offered, wanting to hear an exciting tale instead of a dirge.[4]

"I suppose Jake best tell you about that," Moody said. "Frankly, I've killed so many men I can no longer keep track of them."

"I'm wondering," Daniel began after a few minutes, "if you don't mind my asking, but does that bother a person some? You know, killing so many people?"

Moody cast the young man a direful glance. "Can't speak for others. But me? I don't give a damn about the men I've sent to hell. It's where they belonged."

An hour later Moody directed his horse to a small country store and dismounted. "Remember, keep your trap closed," he warned as the deputy tied his horse to the hitching rail. "You might learn a thing or two."

They entered the one-room store, and from habit Moody quickly glanced around the room. One older, unarmed man sat by a small wood-burning stove and a younger woman, more like a girl on second

---

[4] *High Country Killers, Book IV*

look, busily moved items about on a shelf. Moody watched her eyes widen and a fearful look pass over her face when she saw them. He noticed that she reached into her apron pocket to reassure herself that a weapon was still in there.

"May I help you?" she asked, moving quickly behind the counter.

"Good morning," Moody said, trying to smile pleasantly. "You got any coffee in that pot sitting on that stove? I could sure use a cup." Turning to Daniel, he asked, "How about you, Daniel? You want a cup of coffee?"

Daniel seemed unable to take his eyes off the girl, but finally mumbled an answer.

"Make that two cups, Miss."

As the girl moved from behind the counter to fetch the coffee, Moody hurriedly made his badge more visible and motioned for Daniel to do the same.

"That'll be twenty cents," the girl said, putting the cups on the counter and quickly stepping back.

Moody put a silver dollar on the countertop. "Keep the change," he said in an attempt to put the girl at ease by trying to show that he and Daniel weren't after money.

"I'm Deputy Richard Moody," Richard finally said to the wide-eyed girl. "This here's Deputy U.S. Marshal Daniel Cleary. We're wanting to get some information about the two men who kidnapped a young woman and apparently also robbed this store."

A look of relief swept over the girl's face. "Yes, sir. I can help you. My name is Josephine." She paused a moment, "You'll have to forgive my nervousness. I'm trying to forget about what happened, but it just seems to be branded in my brain."

"That's understandable," Richard replied in the softest tone he could muster. "What can you tell me?"

"Well, sir, they were just awful men. Awful. The one man wasn't quite as awful as the one who actually grabbed me and threatened to do horrible things to me," she replied, her face flushing deeply.

"Did you get their names?"

"Oh, yes. The awful, awful man was named Floyd. The other man was Jarvis. It was Floyd who kidnapped me and then later shot my fiancé."

"You seem might young to be engaged," Daniel blurted.

Moody rolled his eyes at the deputy's comment.

"I'm fifteen and will be sixteen come May," Josephine said indignantly.

"How about last names?" Moody asked.

"I can't rightly remember. I'm not sure I heard their last names. I was so scared."

"So, they just came in the store here and grabbed you?" Moody asked.

"Oh, no. They beat up Grandpa something awful. I was in the back doing my studies when I heard this shouting and commotion. So, I came on in here and the man named Floyd was beating Grandpa with the butt of his gun. It was horrible," Josephine said, her eyes welling with tears at the memory. "The sound of the gun hitting his head just was the most sickening, awful sound I've ever heard."

At this news, Daniel shook his head. "No young woman should ever see or hear anything like that!" he exclaimed, his voice heavy with emotion.

Moody cast another glance at his partner, and then continued. "What happened then, Josephine?"

"Well, Grandpa's head was bleeding and he'd fallen to one knee, but then he completely collapsed. I thought he was dead! There was so much blood! I screamed and grabbed the stick we use to get things off high shelves and ran around the counter to hit the man. Meanwhile, that outlaw shot George Murphy in the shoulder and that knocked George down," she explained and then pointed toward the woodstove. "That's George there by the stove."

"Where's your grandpa?" Moody asked.

"He's still recovering from the beating. The doctor said he may never be the same," Josephine replied, tears now trickling down her cheeks.

Moody could sense that Daniel would hug the girl in sympathy if given half a chance. "Josephine, did the men hurt anyone else hereabouts?"

"Not that I know of," she answered, wiping her tears away, "except they killed my fiancé. We were to be married when I turned 18." Josephine sobbed several times. "I'm sorry for crying. I know it makes me look foolish," she said, her voice quavering as a new rush of tears flowed.

"Nonsense," Daniel said offering her a soiled handkerchief. "Anybody would cry, and nothing could make you look foolish!"

"Are you looking to arrest these men?" she asked holding onto the handkerchief tightly.

"Yes, we are, and you can be assured they'll be caught," Daniel responded, rising to his full height and puffing out his chest.

"Thank you," Josephine said, blushing. "I didn't think any lawmen would bother since I escaped unharmed and was rescued. And Grandpa is old. You know how anymore most folks don't care all that much about the elderly."

Before Daniel could blurt out anything else inane, Moody said, "Josephine, the man who did this is wanted for a lot of crimes. He'll be caught – either by us or another lawman. It may take a bit of time. Meanwhile, do you know how to use that weapon in your pocket?"

Josephine looked down. "I do. Papa taught me to shoot."

"You use that if those men come in here again. Don't hesitate. But whatever happens, don't miss! It'd be better if someone else was in here with you for the time being, instead of George," Moody said, nodding toward the man dozing by the stove.

"My brother is here usually, but right now he's helping Dad with the hay."

"Your family got a ranch?" Daniel asked.

"We own a section."

"Maybe I can come on down from Prescott come harvest time and give you a hand," Daniel offered. "I use to work on a ranch."

Josephine smiled demurely. "That'd be right nice. But aren't you awful busy catching bad men?"

It was Daniel's turn to blush. "Reckon so," he finally said as Moody backed him out the door.

"You certainly know how to make yourself look stupid, Daniel, I'll give you that," Moody commented as he mounted up.

"Well, it isn't right what happened to that girl," Daniel said angrily.

"I thought you were going to propose to her on the spot," Moody replied.

Jarvis McKinney led Floyd Baker on a circuitous route bypassing the communities that lay between themselves and the Colorado River along Arizona's western border. Jarvis didn't want to take any chances that a lawdog would be on the lookout for them. He didn't know how far the news of their crime had spread. Surprised they hadn't been apprehended in the day or two immediately following the robbery and beating of the old man and the kidnapping of the young girl, Jarvis began to relax as the miles between him and the crimes grew. It was four days before they reached Mojave, however, and by this time Floyd Baker had become almost unbearable.

The men camped that night not far from the river and a small encampment of Mojave Indians. They were so close to the Indian encampment, that they could see a faint glow from the fires when it grew dark.

"I'm thinking I might just sneak on over to that Indian camp and find me a woman," Baker commented.

"Not a good idea, Floyd. We don't need any more trouble. We got enough already."

"Pshaw. Ain't nobody comin' after us, Jarvis. I swear you're like a little old lady, always worryin' about nothin'. Besides, no one cares about them squaws."

"Well, I'm thinkin' maybe those people in the tribe might care. And there's a sight more of them than there is of us."

Floyd stood and sniffed as he looked longingly toward the Mojave encampment. "Don't wait up for me, Grandma."

Jarvis shook his head as Floyd mounted up and left. He pondered leaving then and there and abandoning Baker. Jarvis had no doubt the man would be the death of him. Still, he might need Baker in a pinch. There'd be time later to kill him, if the Indians didn't do it first.

It was still dark but nearing dawn when Jarvis awoke. He looked quickly around the campsite and saw Baker's horse hobbled and standing by his own horse. After a few moments he saw Baker.

"About time you woke up," Baker commented. "The sun's almost up and here we sit waitin' to get scalped."

"Ah jeez, Floyd. What happened?"

"What happened is that squaw damn near kicked me to death before I got her down and had my way with her. She almost bit my ear off when I was doin' her. I punched her a good one and that quieted her for a bit, but as soon as I rolled off her she let out a yowl that 'bout raised the dead. Surprised you didn't hear it."

Jarvis thought for a few moments. "No. I didn't hear anything."

"Well, maybe them Indians didn't either then. Anyway, she left me no choice but to cut her damn throat. I sliced her up pretty good – like she was a rare steak. I got started and just kept goin'. I always wanted to do that to someone, you know. Now I done it. It's a good feeling, I gotta say."

"Where's the body?" Jarvis asked nervously.

"Over yonder," Baker replied, nodding toward a scrawny creosote bush.

Jarvis could make out a small mound beside the bush. "You brought her back *here*?"

"Had to. Couldn't leave here where I killed her or the Indians would've found her. I dragged her back here behind my horse. I had quite a time, Jarvis," Baker said, grinning evilly.

Jarvis arose quickly. Now there would be a trail, and the Indians would likely find it. They weren't used as scouts for the military for no reason.

"We gotta get out of here, Floyd. Pack up."

"Don't be in such a rush, Jarvis. I plan on goin' back and gettin' another squaw. A young one this time. I'll bring her back here tonight and we can have us a good time."

"Damn it, Floyd!" Jarvis stood, exasperated and uncertain whether to shoot the monster before him or not. Baker's gun belt lay on the ground beside him. He'd be easy to take. "I'm leaving. You can stay as long as you want," Jarvis said, turning and letting the opportunity slip by.

After a few moments, Baker secured his horse and began saddling.

The two men veered in a southeasterly direction away from the river and the Mojave encampment and rode for several hours before stopping. Jarvis knew a scout with any ability would be able to track them, but he felt better having some mileage behind him.

Baker shot a jack rabbit that afternoon, so they stopped to build a small fire and have a bite. "How far we going today?"

"As far as we can," Jarvis answered. "The farther the better."

"Thought you said we was gonna rob and kill a bunch of crazy, rich old miners."

"We will."

"When?"

Exasperated, Jarvis answered, "Today, Floyd. We'll find someone today. We'll get their food, maybe a burro to pack it on, and any gold they have on them."

Baker nodded eagerly in response.

Late that afternoon Floyd Baker saw what he'd been waiting for. A lone miner with a string of three burros had made camp in the shade of an overhanging rock at the base of a small mountain. Even from a distance, the men could see a pile of packs scattered on the ground. Nothing but desolation stretched in all directions, but a small canyon barely visible in the opening of the rock wall where the miner camped showed vegetation.

"Probably water in that green break in the canyon wall," Jarvis mused. "These horses need to drink. So do I," he said, shaking his empty canteen.

"Well, let's go meet our new friend and give him his last rites," Baker said as he started to draw his gun.

"Put that damn thing away, Floyd. You think he ain't armed? Think again. If he sees you riding up with a gun in hand, he's likely to blow both of us to kingdom come. He might be old or not, but it don't mean he's dumb. You gotta ride up there nice and friendly like."

Distances in the desert are deceiving, so it was early evening before the two outlaws rode into Henry Hillsdale's camp. The wary old miner reluctantly let the men water their mounts.

"You best be on your way now," Hillsdale said. "There's a good spot to camp about a quarter mile farther along. You can't miss it. There's been plenty of folks who've camped there. It's a full moon tonight, so if you keep an eye out you'll see a large fire pit."

"Not very hospitable are you, old man?" Baker asked, scowling.

"Person can't afford to be in my line of work," Hillsdale replied, hoisting a shotgun.

"Now, that gun there won't be necessary, mister," Jarvis said.

In the moment that Hillsdale glanced toward Jarvis, Baker drew his weapon and shot the old man between the eyes.

"Get his body out of here," Jarvis directed as he dismounted.

Baker proceeded to drag Hillsdale's body every which way behind his horse for twenty minutes or better. He left the prospector laying in the desert, a feast for vultures.

"That old geezer didn't have a lick of skin or clothing left on him," Baker said after he returned to the miner's campsite. "Thanks for lettin' me do that, Jarvis. You're okay. I take back them things I said about you bein' an old lady."

Jarvis smiled and nodded. Baker's absence had given him an opportunity to look through some of Hillsdale's belongings for any gold the miner might have found. He'd found a nice stash in the old man's tent, along with a bottle of whiskey.

Jarvis held up the bottle for Baker to see, and a mile-wide grin spread across the outlaw's face.

After going through several more of Hillsdale's packs, they found two more bottles of whiskey, and Baker was beside himself. "You had a good idea, Jarvis. A real good idea to come here and rob these old coots."

Jarvis drank very little, but Baker knew no limits. For three days Baker drank. At first he was jovial, but then he grew mean. That's the way it had always been. But during the times that Baker lay passed out, Jarvis continued going through Hillsdale's packs. He found letters written by a woman begging Henry to come home. And he found a piece of gold jewelry in a small gift box with a ribbon on it. Apparently the old man had not mailed it, or he was saving it for a soiled dove. Now, thought Jarvis, I'll have a nice brooch to give to the woman I marry, and he packed it and along with few small leather sacks of gold dust in with his own gear.

The buzzards swarmed Hillsdale's corpse during the day, and coyotes slunk in at nightfall. Within three days scarcely a remnant of Henry Hillsdale remained.

"Time to move on, Floyd," Jarvis said on the fourth morning, nudging the hungover man with his toe. "We been here must be goin' on four or five days. We gotta be on the move. We've gorged ourselves on the old man's food and there ain't hardly any left."

"Shoot one of them noisy asses," Floyd mumbled, trying to open his bloodshot eyes.

Jarvis didn't take to killing animals, though. Once he started saddling his horse, Floyd slowly sat up and looked around.

"Jeez I hate this place. Hey! Let's go get us another woman."

"Sure, Floyd. Let's go get a woman. We'll be in Yuma in a few days and you can spend a whole week in a brothel. It's on me."

There could be no greater motivation for Floyd Baker.

7.

Heading southwest out of Yuma, Baker and McKinney had easy going for a spell, but soon ran into Colorado River delta muck that neither man had had the foresight to anticipate. It took them better than two weeks to slog their way through the marshy land to San Felipe. The horses got bogged down in the marshy delta created by the Colorado River flowing into the Sea of Cortez, and at times it seemed the ground might swallow them whole and be the end of them. Despite Baker's continuous cursing, McKinney forged on. There was no turning back. After countless days of struggling through mire, the land finally dried considerably, and the trip went better until Baker's horse went lame.

"You can't beat on an animal and expect it to obey you, Floyd," an exasperated McKinney shouted at the sweating, swearing Baker as the man viciously jerked on his horse's bridle while trying to beat its hindquarters with his pistol. "The horse plum can't walk no more."

"You shut up, Jarvis, before I use this gun to beat on you," Floyd threatened.

Between the heat and his hunger, Baker quickly ran out of steam. Disgusted with his predicament, he shot the horse, emptying his gun into the suffering animal.

"Now, how you gonna get to San Felipe?" Jarvis dared to ask, fearing the answer before he even finished the question. "At least when he was living he might've limped along with you. Or you could've used him for trade or somethin'."

"Give me your horse, Jarvis," Baker demanded.

"No, siree. You done shot your horse, now you're gonna walk," Jarvis replied, reluctantly pulling his weapon from its holster.

The two men faced each other, each with gun in hand. Jarvis mounted on his horse, Baker on foot. After a tense moment, Baker remembered his gun was empty and he holstered the weapon. "Hell, I'll just steal me the first horse we come across."

"That's a fine idea," Jarvis said, relieved at how the episode had ended, yet hesitating to holster his weapon. He knew that Baker was also good with a knife, which he wore on his belt.

"I don't even care if it's a plug-ugly nag. I just want to get to San Felipe and have a beer and a woman. You still payin' for all this?"

Jarvis smiled and nodded. *I'm paying until some fed-up Mex kills you,* he thought. *That should only take a day or two once they figure you out for the savage meat ax you are.*

Jarvis still had plenty of money remaining that he'd lifted from Henry Hillsdale and two other miners he and Baker robbed and murdered on their killing spree to Yuma. He figured he had enough money to support himself for a long spell – if he didn't have to pay for Baker's damages, anyway.

Fortunately for Baker, the ground almost completely dried, so walking became considerably easier. "Do they play cards in Mexico?" Baker asked one afternoon.

"I reckon they do. Maybe not cards like we play, but I'm sure they gamble. Most everyone in the whole world gambles. Everyone that I know, anyway," Jarvis answered.

"Good. 'Cause I'm a good card player. I can make us a lot of money that'll buy as much women and whiskey as we'll ever want."

"Gotta be careful about winnin' too much, Floyd. Them Mexicans will slit your throat. You gotta lose a hand once in a while," Jarvis advised, knowing full well that Baker was a notorious card cheat.

"How much farther?"

"Not far," Jarvis answered, having no idea of the distance. "We'll stop at that little shack I see up ahead and take a rest. Maybe spend the night."

"I hope they got some women there."

"Floyd, you gotta be on good behavior until we know if they have guns. I'm bettin' they do, bein' out here alone and all."

"Well, I don't care. If they got a gun, I'm takin' it. And if they got a horse, I'm takin' it, too."

Somehow always a day or two behind Baker and McKinney, Richard Moody and Daniel Cleary followed the string of bodies left by the outlaws to Yuma. No matter how far and hard Moody pushed the horses, it seemed like the two outlaws were always just out of reach.

"How the hell are they staying ahead of us?" an exhausted Cleary complained.

"That's the best question you've asked yet," Moody finally responded. "Beats the hell out of me. All I can figure is they have to be stealing fresh mounts regularly. Ours are about spent. Between the heat, the scant food, and the long days, they don't have much left."

"So what're we going to do?"

"We'll leave these in Yuma for the time being and get some new animals."

"Can we at least stay long enough in Yuma to take a bath? I stink and my clothes are stiff with sweat."

"I've been telling you night after night to take a swim in the river," Moody chided the young man.

Cleary looked away, reddening. Moody suspected Cleary was unwilling to confess that he couldn't swim. Moody wasn't much of a swimmer himself, and the current had been swift and the water frigid, but somehow he'd taken a quick dip every evening that they'd camped by the river. "We'll stay a day or two in Yuma. Rest up. I could use some good food. Plus I need to take care of some business."

"Then what? We heading back?"

Moody's withering look said it all.

"So now we're following these guys where? California?"

"No. They'll most likely head into Mexico if they haven't already."

"Mexico? You don't mean the place where all those Mexicans live who speak another language, I hope."

"That's the place."

"Moody, what are you thinking? We don't have jurisdiction down there!" Daniel Cleary wearily plopped down, slowing shaking his head in disbelief. "I'm gonna have to wire Jake about this. I'm not following you down there, and that's all there is to it."

"I told you before, Daniel, you're welcome to go back. Go or stay. It makes no difference to me. In fact, it's best you go on back. I have Baker to kill along with some unfinished business down there. You stand a grand chance of being killed if you tag along." Moody suspected Diego Fuentes would quickly learn of his arrival and would want to settle the score regarding Margaret. He knew the showdown between him and Fuentes was a matter of the Mexican's pride, not love for the woman.

Cleary quickly stood and stomped off, muttering a string of curses. He stopped after a few feet and turned, "You know what, Moody? You are certifiably crazy. Crazy as a loon." Then he continued to the river, sputtering and swearing.

An hour later as Moody sat propped against his saddle watching the sunset, Daniel returned from the river. "Damn that water's cold," the young man said.

"Yes, it is."

After a few minutes of silence, Cleary asked, "So, what's the problem you have in Mexico?"

"It's a long story," Moody said. "And it's past your bedtime."

"Listen, you ass! I'm sick of being treated like a kid. I'm a grown man and a Deputy U.S. Marshal, not some cheap gunslinger for hire," Cleary snapped.

Moody inhaled deeply, then sighed. "That's fair, I suppose."

"So, what's the story?"

It was several more minutes before Moody answered. "Basically, a Mexican named Diego Fuentes and I both loved the same woman. I stole her back after Fuentes bought her from a fisherman who found her, barely alive, floating on storm debris in the ocean. Fuentes didn't take kindly to that. Margaret and I escaped while Jake held Fuentes and his small army off. Jake got shot to hell and nearly died, and he would have died had Fuentes not decided to save his life. Fuentes held Jake captive for a long time," Moody said in a low voice, staring at the small embers in the fire.[5] "Eventually I came to my senses and went back to Mexico to find out what happened to Jake and to kill Fuentes. Jake and I met up, by sheer luck, in Ensenada. We tried escaping but the Mexican quickly trailed us. We got real lucky, though, and got away after a skirmish with Fuentes and one of his men. We left Fuentes in the desert without a horse. The man vowed to kill us both."[6]

Clearly sat with his mouth open, eyes wide. "You have to be making this up!"

"Every word is true, and there's more, but Jake can fill you in on that."

"Why didn't you just kill the Mexican and leave him in the desert?"

"I was all for that, but Jake has a sense of 'loyalty,' I guess you could say. He refused to kill Fuentes because the man had saved his life."

"Well, I never!" Cleary exclaimed.

---

[5] *Back from the Dead, Book V*

[6] *Gunslinger Justice, Book VI*

"It gets better, an Indian – an Apache – showed up a day later and basically rescued us after we'd run out of water and the horse we'd stolen went lame. That's another man Jake should have killed but spared."[7]

Mesmerized by the adventure, Cleary remained speechless for a long spell.

The following afternoon the two lawmen rode into Yuma. Though hot and dusty, the town seemed an oasis to the weary men. After putting their mounts up at the stable, Moody paid for two rooms at a hotel and ordered up baths. "It's on me, kid," he casually remarked. For once, Cleary didn't argue.

Though tired and hungry, Moody wasted no time in talking with the local sheriff about Baker and McKinney.

"Yep. They was here, okay. I'm pretty sure I know who you're talkin' about if one of 'em is so ugly it hurts to look at 'im. I ran 'em out of town. Told 'em if they wanted to stay free men, they best be on their way," the sheriff said.

"They cause any trouble? Break any laws?"

"Not exactly yes…and not exactly no," the sheriff answered. "The ugly one plum tore up the whorehouse. Beat one of the girls pretty bad. I only let them go because the other one paid for the damages. The business folks stopped selling to them, and after I had a little chat with the fellows, they agreed to leave town."

"How long ago did they leave?" Moody asked, dreading the answer.

"Two days ago. Maybe three. They skipped out on the hotel bill, too. If they come back, I'll put 'em behind bars, that's certain."

---

[7] *Apache, Book II*

"Well, I wish you'd have done that this time," Moody said, frowning.

"I don't need no tin-star deputy second-guessing me, Mister. I got a full house here. If there'd been room for another hooligan, I'd have locked 'em up. Their crimes weren't capital as far as I was concerned," the sheriff retorted. "If I arrested every cowhand who got overly excited in a whorehouse, I'd have to build a new jail every month. Now, if you'll excuse me, I got some business to attend to."

"Wait," Moody said. "What's the ugly one's partner look like? Did you get a good look at him?"

"He was a quiet one. Easy to overlook. As I recall he wasn't real big, but you could tell he was strong. Stocky type. Blue-eyed fella. Wore a big, black hat, but I'm guessin' he had brown hair since he had a brown beard. Seemed like he was the smart one of the two."

"Do you happen to know where they headed?" Moody asked, standing to leave.

"No idea, but I'd bet on Mexico."

"What makes you think that?"

"It's what their type usually does. I see it weekly. They head on down there and raise havoc until the military strings 'em up or shoots 'em…if they can catch 'em."

"Here's some money to take the train back to Prescott," Moody said when Cleary joined him for dinner.

"What about my horse?" Cleary asked.

"That horse is spent, Daniel, but if you insist, give it a week's worth of recuperation and then take a slow ride back. Use the money how you want."

"Well, what if I tell you I'm going with you?"

"That's not a good decision, kid."

"Yeah, I know. It's my worst idea yet, but this trip has been a river of bad ideas, so why change things now? Besides, I've never been to Mexico and probably won't ever go if I don't go now."

"If you go now, Daniel, it may be the last time you go anywhere," Moody said. "Stop and think, and then go back to Prescott."

"Damn you, Moody. I'm going. I'm a grown man, and when I say I'm going, you aren't going to stop me. I was not born in the woods to be scared by an owl, you know."

Richard cut a piece of steak and slowly chewed it. Finally he said, "Suit yourself. I'm taking the train to San Diego tomorrow. I've got some business to take care of. I'll cross into Mexico from there. If you want to go with me, the train leaves at 8:00."

"Don't go sneaking off in the morning without me, either. Don't try that old trick. I plan on going the whole hog with you."

"I won't sneak off. After I take care of my business, we'll buy some horses and then head into Mexico."

"How long this 'business' of yours gonna take?" Daniel asked.

"Two days at most, I expect."

"I've never been to San Diego either," Daniel commented after a few moments. "Say, are we going to run into that Fuentes man when we're down there in Mexico?"

"Most likely. He's the biggest toad in the puddle. He pretty much controls Baja Norte."

"What's that?"

"Northern Mexico."

"Where do we look for the two outlaws down there? You know where they are?"

"Right now they're most likely in one of two places," Moody said. "Either Tijuana or San Felipe. Both towns are known for the no-accounts that cross the border to hide out."

"You going to let Jake know where we're going?"

Moody looked up.

“I think it’s a good idea he knows. Maybe he’ll come on down and help us. I’ll send a telegram tomorrow,” Daniel said.

“I’ll take care of that before we leave in the morning. That’s a good idea,” Richard offered, although he had no intention of doing so.

“You know,” Daniel said, after a few minutes of forking food into his mouth, “I’m kind of looking forward to this. I bet I’ll have pretty good stories to tell when this is all over.”

Moody only shook his head in response.

“I mean, you and Jake, now you guys got stories that I could listen to all day and all night. I want some stories to tell.”

“I only hope you live to tell them, Daniel.”

Diego Fuentes sat in the back of a small cantina in Ensenada, Mexico. He took a long drag on his cigar and slowly exhaled the smoke. Rolling the cigar in his fingers, he studied the red embers. “This is good, Raul. Very good. Send for boxes of these.”

“Si, Senor Fuentes.”

“Now, what news of my Arizona gringo?”

“Senor Fuentes, Jake Silver stays always the same. He makes no changes or movements to cross the border.”

Diego sagely nodded his head and sat in thought for a full five minutes before speaking. “So, he is still the U.S. Marshal. Now I must ask myself again and again, what kind of man would not avenge the death of his woman?”

“Senor, it is rumored that Silver waits for the time. And, of most importance, my informant tells me that he has heard Silver say that another man killed his woman, not you. So there would be no reason for him to come for you,” Raul said, nervously shifting from foot to foot.

"Another man?" Diego's interest piqued. "Well, that's a pity. I was hoping to see Silver again. I have unfinished business with him."

"Yes, Senor. *But,*" and Raul emphasized the word for effect, "Juan Pablo has sent word that the gringo who stole your woman is returning to Mexico." Raul positively beamed with pride that he'd been able to give Fuentes a striking piece of news. "He is even now in Yuma."

"Moody? The gringo Richard Moody will return? You are certain?"

"Si, Senor. Juan Pablo says that Moody and another man are likely following two Americanos. Bad men, both. And the desperados are in San Felipe, or very near, at last report."

A small smile crossed Diego's face as he tossed some pesos to Raul. "You have given me good news, Raul. Come back when you have more. Don't forget about Jake Silver, though. I want to know every move my gringo friend makes."

Raul slowly backed out the door, nodding in appreciation – and relief – that the meeting with the big man had ended.

Diego stood and slowly paced around the mostly empty cantina. He had his second, Angel Sanchez, shoo the stragglers from the room. The big man needed quiet to think about the news that Richard Moody dared return to Baja Norte, his empire. Many thoughts flooded the Mexican's mind – memories of the beautiful Margarita who'd been kidnapped then rescued from drowning at sea, then kidnapped again by Moody and Silver. The two gringos had outfoxed him and left him on foot in the desert. Diego could almost forgive Jake Silver – a man he'd come to regard as perhaps his best friend, but Silver had betrayed him and would ultimately have to pay. Never, though, would he forgive the measly Richard Moody, a small man who wore spectacles!

Diego felt a bit of relief, however, knowing that the death of Silver's woman was not being blamed on him. "Silver knows I am an honorable man and that I would never stoop to such a killing," Diego muttered to no one but himself. The Mexican prided himself on the fact that he only killed those who betrayed him. He'd have killed his Margarita for such a betrayal had he gotten her back, but rumor from a reliable source had informed him that Margarita had died in Arizona, something other informants later verified. "Moody must die for stealing my woman and making a fool of me!" Diego said loudly.

Diego had to find out who the men were that Moody and the other gringo pursued. Obviously bad men. He hoped the outlaws would not kill Moody before he had a chance to do so. He'd send some men to San Felipe to ferret out the gringos and to keep them there should they think of moving on. In San Felipe, Diego would finally get to send Moody to hell.

A plan began to form, and Diego walked decisively through the cantina's batwing doors. "Where's Alfonso?" he shouted. Turning to another of his men he ordered, "Find Alfonso." To yet another he commanded, "Get me a small remuda and prepare to leave tomorrow for San Felipe. Tell Juan, Martinez, Fabio, and Fernando that they leave for San Felipe with me. Tell them to make ready and meet with me at the Casa Ensenada tonight."

Diego strode quickly to the hotel-like accommodations which only he and his men occupied when he traveled to Ensenada from his hacienda in Guerrero Negro. He felt almost buoyant as he thought about killing Richard Moody. He loved a good man-hunt. He contemplated torturing the gunman to death instead of sending a bullet into his heart. He liked the idea of skinning the scrawny bastard alive and then castrating him for a grand finale. He'd leave Moody hanging in the town's square as a warning to others who thought they could steal from him and get away with it. He smiled broadly as he entered the Casa Ensenada. His smile always struck fear into those who knew him. Fuentes ruled Baja Norte with an iron fist. He had an army of murderers and informants, and at all times he knew what was transpiring and who was not honoring him. People paid dearly for even their thoughts. He viewed himself as a parental figure to the child-like populace.

8

Moody's business in San Diego took longer than he expected. Though exasperated by the delay, he knew that Baker and McKinney would likely stay put wherever they happened to land in Mexico. They'd committed too many crimes to consider crossing back into the country any time soon. He tried to think of the layover in San Diego as a final rest before plunging into Diego Fuentes' territory.

Cleary, however, seemed to enjoy himself and spent his time wandering about the picturesque town, giving Moody a rundown every evening of the sites he'd seen.

A week after their arrival, Moody had finally established an account at a San Diego bank and left explicit instructions about the partial disbursement of the available funds if, and only if, his nephew Buddy Reed showed up with enough evidence to prove his identity. Although the banker expressed reservations about this unorthodox arrangement, and let Moody know that he was extremely uncomfortable with the responsibility of handling the situation, Moody made it worthwhile for the man.

Business finished, Moody spent an afternoon picking out three good-looking horses; two to ride, and one to pack gear for the trip.

"You'd think we were gonna be gone for a month," Cleary exclaimed, looking at the panniers and articles to be packed.

"It's not too late for you to go back," Moody replied. "I just remember all too well scrounging for food and water in the desert. Don't care to do that again if I can help it."

"Well, what if we catch 'em the first day?"

"Nothing would make me happier."

"Is Jake going to pay you back for all the money you've spent?" Cleary asked, a concerned look on his face.

"Probably not. It won't matter, so don't worry yourself," Moody replied, cinching the packs securely with rope. "You ready?"

"We leaving right now? Right this minute?"

"You have something else to do? More sight-seeing?"

"No, I guess not. I'll get my gear."

The two men rode several hours that afternoon before renting a room in a rundown establishment. Moody paid several questionable characters a handful of pesos to watch the horses and gear.

"Are you sure you can trust these people with our stuff?" Cleary asked. "They don't look too trustworthy to me."

"Money talks here, Daniel."

Cleary had a bundle of questions about how to locate the men and what to do when they found them. Moody left most of the questions unanswered.

Moody scoured Tijuana for three days, but there was no indication the culprits had been there. He also could feel the eyes of Fuentes' spies on him. The big man himself was nowhere to be seen, but that didn't make him any less attentive.

That night as they were finishing their dinners in a small cantina, Moody became aware of a man standing a few feet from the table, scrutinizing them. The stranger came forward when Richard looked up and nodded.

"Senor, for the interruption I apologize."

Moody studied the Mexican closely, wondering if he and Jake might have had a run-in with the man on their previous foray south of the border.

"The men you are looking for are now in San Felipe."

"Who sent you to tell me this?" Moody asked.

"Senor, we both know who sent me."

"So. The showdown will be in San Felipe." Moody stated, rather than asked.

"Si, Senor." The man backed away, casting a menacing look at the two men.

"Who the heck was that?" Cleary asked.

"An emissary from Fuentes. Baker and McKinney are in San Felipe."

"Yeah. I got that part. I don't like the sounds of the showdown part, though."

"It's still not too late to go back, Daniel."

"Well, I'm ready to go somewhere. This town is disturbing," Daniel said, pushing his plate away. "It's disorganized, not to mention dirty. All that jibber-jabber. Why don't they just talk American, like us? A lot of poor people and a lot of bad-looking hombres in this town."

"That your new word? Hombre?" Moody teased as he laid a small pile of pesos on the table.

"How far is this San Felipe?" Daniel asked.

"You know all those supplies we packed? They'll be gone before we arrive."

"Don't these people believe in train travel?"

It only took a week before Floyd Baker and Jarvis McKinney were known throughout the small settlement of San Felipe. Despite McKinney's urging to stay in the background and not attract attention to himself, Baker quickly became notorious. He drank heavily and grabbed at every girl who passed by. Filthy, abusive, and bleary-eyed, he stayed drunk so long that McKinney hoped the man would die of his own accord.

Neither man noticed the small group of well-armed Mexicans who seemed to follow wherever they ventured. It was the four soldiers' job to watch the two Americanos until Fuentes arrived and to make sure the gringos did not leave San Felipe. Diego had given strict orders on that account. At times, Baker even gambled with one or two of the men, and no matter how loudly he talked or cursed at them, they did not respond to his attempts to teach them poker.

McKinney, more circumspect, rarely drank and spent even less time whoring and carousing. He whiled away his time slowly strolling up and down the sandy streets and often along the water's edge. He liked the water and enjoyed watching the small fishing boats go out in the mornings and return in the evenings with full nets. McKinney had never been around a body of water that he couldn't see across, and it took a great deal of time and hand gestures for a local to convince McKinney that the water he was seeing was not the Pacific Ocean.

"No Pacifico. *"El golfo,"* the man repeated many times. "The gulf."

McKinney bought the man's straw hat, exchanging his own well-worn black one along with a handful of pesos which seemed like play money to him.

The big trouble for the two arose on a Friday night when many local *campesinos* came to town to drink and spend their hard-earned pesos. Baker, irritated by the throng of babbling Mexicans crowding the bar, fired his pistol several times into the air. The noise scared and deafened most everyone in the room, and a bullet struck a candle chandelier, causing a burning candle to fall onto a table piled high with dirty cards. Baker's unintelligible cursing and shouting raised the ire of nearly every man present, and before he knew what was happening, he found himself on the dirt floor with half a dozen raggedy men on top of him wrapping a rope around his legs and viciously punching and kicking him. They dragged him out the door despite the hullabaloo he raised, and tied the rope to a burro that took off down the street after being smacked soundly on its rear. The burro, frightened by the screaming, flailing object behind it, moved all the faster. Finally knocked unconscious, Baker fell silent and eventually, tiring of dragging its load, the little donkey stopped running. McKinney hauled Baker's limp body back to town.

The half dead Baker was bed-prone for days, a battered mess. McKinney suspected, and hoped, the man's end was at hand.

"I heard what happened to your friend a few days ago. Too bad. These Mexicans can get a mite bit ornery if provoked," a stranger said as he took a place by McKinney at the bar.

McKinney straightened and turned to see another American. "Good to hear someone say something I can understand," McKinney said, smiling broadly. "You're a welcome sight, stranger."

"Oh, I'm no stranger in these parts. I've been living here a few years now. Ben McGraw's the name," the man said, extending his hand.

"I'm Jarvis McKinney. Pleased to meet you," Jarvis responded, pumping the man's hand in a hearty shake. "Good to hear someone talk American!"

"So, what brings you and your partner down to these parts?" McGraw asked.

McKinney smiled. "The law. What else?"

"You plan on sticking around?"

"Only as long as I have to."

"Let's get a table and talk."

McGraw paid for a bottle of tequila, and the two men moved through the crowd to a small table in the back. It didn't take long for McKinney to recite the litany of crimes he and Baker had committed. "Problem is, Baker is out of his mind most of the time. He's a dangerous man," McKinney said. "I'm no saint, but that man is the devil's own son."

McGraw nodded. "So, what's your plan? You sticking around here and marrying a Mex, or planning on returning?"

"Well, I never thought about marryin' a Mex, now that you mention it. But most likely I'll end up goin' back. I'm thinking Baker will die from bein' dragged like that. I could go on to Californy by myself and probably be just fine," McKinney answered, realizing that what he'd just said made perfect sense even though he'd never considered going to California before saying it. "What about you? What keeps you here?"

McGraw smiled. "I'm alive. I won't be for long if I go back."

"You must've done something purty darn bad."

McGraw nodded. "I did. Sometimes I almost regret it. Then I come to my senses and remember how that bitch shot my son and killed him. She didn't even stand trial for it. Someone else took the blame and got off scot-free."

"Why'd she kill your boy?" McKinney asked.

"She married my boy, then cuckolded him. The woman was a tramp. I'll admit my boy back-shot the man she loved, and I'll admit the man was a good person and had been a good friend of mine for many years, except for the fact that he slept with my boy's wife." McGraw took a long drink.

"Did the man your boy shot die?"

"No. No, he did not."

"So, what's the problem? Granted your boy, God rest his soul, is departed, but why would you die?"

"Because I shot the woman." McGraw's face filled with misery. "I shot her in the head. Right in front of the man and their daughter."

At a loss for words for a few moments, McKinney took a long drink, then finally said, "Well, that don't mean the man's gonna hunt you down and kill you."

"That man was Marshal Jake Silver."

McKinney almost choked on his drink. Both men sat without talking for a few minutes. Then McKinney asked, "Well, does he know where you are?"

"He probably does. Not sure why he hasn't come yet, unless it's because of his daughter. But he'll come. He'll come."

"Well, Ben, you got more than a pile of trouble. Worse than me and Baker. I've heard of Jake Silver. He's got a reputation that stretches from here to the Mississippi. Him and a sidekick that use to ride with him killed more'n nine men once," McKinney said. "And I heard the guy that rode with him is a hired gun. Kills people for money. Now, that's a job to have," McKinney said, his eyes widening. "What's a marshal doin' runnin' around with a gunslinger, though?"

"They're all the same, Jarvis. All the same. Cut from the same damn cloth."

"Same cloth that we're cut from?"

McGraw chuckled and nodded. After a moment he said, "Listen, I live in a small hacienda south of here. About five miles or so. Come on down and stay a spell. I got a good woman who can cook and clean and keep a man satisfied."

"Just might do that, Ben. Thanks." As an afterthought he asked, "How do you come up with money to pay for all that, anyway?"

"We can talk about that when you come down." McGraw stood and picked up his hat. "Just one thing, Jarvis – don't bring your friend. If you're smart," and Ben looked around the room, "see to it that he doesn't recover or the same thing could happen to you."

Diego Fuentes arrived in San Felipe with a flair. The locals knew who their benefactor, and real governor was, and it wasn't the man who occupied the official position. Fuentes governed Baja Norte with a long arm, a heavy hand, and a large army of 'soldiers'.

Disappointed that Moody and his companion had not yet arrived, Diego settled in to wait. He knew the gunman would not be long. The man had a tenacity that galled him. "He's a brazen, arrogant little man,"

Diego often said of Moody. "He is nothing without Jake Silver by his side." When informed of Baker's unfortunate "accident," Diego summoned the local horse doctor to tend to the man. "He must live so I can be assured of revenge," Diego instructed the terrified man. "If he dies, you die."

No matter how the local medical practitioner tried to explain that Baker was far gone and had suffered severe head injuries and been left untended for too long, Diego would not listen. "He must live, so I can kill Moody!" he roared in fury. "Moody will come for him. The man must not die!"

Fuentes wasted no time in finding out who McKinney was. He received a report from each of his men, and decided McKinney's only value was in drawing Moody to San Felipe. He couldn't help but wonder, though, why Moody would risk so much to track down such men. McKinney was not worth the bullet it would take to kill him. And so Diego spent hours speculating on what McKinney and Baker had, or knew, that caused Moody to risk so much.

Finally, Fuentes sent for McKinney, and after a three-day search his men delivered the frightened man.

"We found him riding into town from the south, from Colonia Gutierrez way," Hugo reported.

McKinney stood before Fuentes, fidgeting with his hat.

Diego said nothing for a spell, but looked McKinney over, disgust registering on his face. "What business do you have in Colonia Gutierrez?" he finally asked.

McKinney's voice cracked as he started to speak. "Just visiting a friend," he replied. "Well, not really a friend," he said, uncertain if the big Mexican liked McGraw or not. "Just moseyin' on down that way and stopped to see a man I met in the cantina. That's all. I swear."

"Ben McGraw is not a good man for you to associate with," Diego said. "You think I am so stupid I do not know who lives in Colonia Gutierrez? You insult me."

"Now, sir, I meant no disrespect. I didn't think it was important is all. That's what I'm trying to say."

Diego Fuentes towered over McKinney. "I decide what is important in this country? Do you understand that? You are not even welcome here. You and your kind come to my country and rob and steal from my people. You drink and whore with our young girls."

McKinney, fearing death was next, decided he would not die a coward. "Now you listen to me. I don't know or care who you are. I ain't done nothin' wrong here. It's true my partner, laying upstairs right now dying, did some foolish things. But I ain't him."

Diego threw back his head and laughed loudly. "The mouse has roared. Well, good for you, but you will die anyway. Not by my hand, but by the man who even now hunts you like the cur you are."

McKinney was perplexed. "Ain't no one huntin' me that I know of."

"Then you are even more foolish than I thought. A man must always be aware of who follows him."

"I think you got me confused, Mister Deego," McKinney said, mispronouncing Diego's name.

"Take this man and have him dig three graves. One for his friend upstairs, one for himself, and one for the hunter, Richard Moody," Diego ordered Hugo. "When he has finished, chain him to the wagon behind the cantina so I can look out my window and watch him die when Moody finds him."

"Mr. Deego, I'll make a deal with you. I got information you'll want to hear. I promise you it'll be worth my life," McKinney cried out in a quavering voice.

Diego studied McKinney's petrified face and doubted the man had any information that would convince him to spare the scoundrel's life. "So, tell me."

"You got to promise you'll not kill me," McKinney said, trying to barter.

"I will decide if your information is worthwhile. I decide. Not you. So now you tell me, or I will cut your tongue out for using it wastefully." Diego withdrew a long, curved knife from a scabbard secured to the side of his thigh. "I have a collection of tongues and ears. Want to see?" and he pulled a small string of what looked like dried tongues from the desk drawer.

McKinney's eyes bugged and his face blanched. He shook so hard he could barely stand without support. Heart pounding, he said, "That man, Ben McGraw, he told me about what he done to Jake Silver's woman. And he told me that Jake Silver made a fool out of you, and that Jake will someday return to Mexico to kill McGraw and you both." McKinney paused. "That's what he told me."

"You have told me nothing new," Diego said, "and you have wasted my time." He nodded to Hugo who took the bound man by the arm and dragged him out the door.

Diego listened to McKinney begging for mercy, but the man's pleas fell on deaf ears. Diego had been stunned at what McKinney had reported. He'd known of Ben McGraw's presence and that the man made a living by buying and selling opium and other items on the black market. Diego had never bothered with McGraw because the man lived with a Mexican woman and had not made a nuisance of himself. But now, knowing that the culprit who had killed Jake's woman lived in his territory, caused Diego to fume. He wanted to kill McKinney, Baker, *and* McGraw immediately. No, not kill them…massacre them. Then he would burn McGraw alive after he tortured the man for hours.

"Fernando," Diego yelled. "Fernando! Here! Now!"

Fernando immediately stood in the doorframe. "Senor."

"Fernando, get the man called Ben McGraw. Bring him here. Do not let him escape. He must be alive when he gets here, although he might have some unexpected accidents, perhaps?"

"Si, Senor Fuentes." Fernando turned to go.

"And Fernando, take someone with you. I do not want this McGraw to escape."

It was not like Diego to act so impulsively, and even though he had vowed to kill Jake Silver should the marshal ever enter his territory, it showed weakness and cowardice beyond anything he could name for any man to kill Jake's woman, or Jake too, for that matter. Even though the marshal had escaped Diego's months-long captivity and had duped him in the desert, Diego had grown to admire him. Indeed, Jake was the only friend he'd ever had.

"Had we not been born on opposite sides of the border, I might have called you brother," Diego once said to Jake. The Mexican was not stupid, and he knew the Americano could easily have killed him at their last meeting in the desert, but instead the lawman, against Moody's strong urging, had left him enough water to make it to the closest settlement. Diego also knew, although he would never admit it aloud, that he could never bring himself to kill Jake Silver. Sometimes, when he was drunk, he could even admit to himself that he missed his friend.

And now – now with the real killer at hand, Diego could let Jake know where McGraw was. Jake would return to kill McGraw, and Diego would take Jake captive again. He would have his brother back.

Thinking of Jake and the many months he'd kept him prisoner in his hacienda, brought back many pleasant memories and calmed the big Mexican. Diego remembered the long dinners the two had eaten in the garden kitchen, drinking and overlooking the ocean. They could talk for hours on any subject. It had been an invigorating time in Diego's life. And the women – he had brought Jake only the most beautiful, nubile young Mexican girls to have as his own, but the man only talked of his woman, a blonde girl named Betsy.

Diego called for some tequila. He lit a cigar and sat in a large easy chair on the upper balcony, watching McKinney bawling like a cow as he attempted to dig three graves in the hard-packed dirt behind the cantina. Of course Diego would not bury anyone there. He would have his men break their legs and then leave Baker and McKinney in the desert to be devoured by vultures, coyotes, and wild dogs. In fact, he decided he'd rid himself of the blubbering McKinney immediately. For Moody, Diego had something else in mind. And for Ben McGraw he would save the very best. He would watch Jake Silver beat the man to death. It would be a beautiful thing to witness. "It's all good. Very, very good," he murmured, smiling happily for the first time in days.

9

The road to San Felipe proved to be a quick and rough education for Daniel Cleary. The young marshal had not fully appreciated the hardships Moody had cautioned him of when they left Tijuana. Three days into the trek Cleary regretted his refusal to return to Prescott.

The first day had served as a warning, but he'd assumed things couldn't get much worse after several horsemen ambushed him and Moody. Despite bullets flying in all directions, neither he nor Moody were injured. After the attack, one Mexican lie dead on the side of the trail, however. The ambushers had very obviously been after the pack horse and supplies. They succeeded only in cutting one of the pack ropes loose instead of Moody's lead rope. It all happened so quickly that Daniel wasn't sure exactly from which direction the men had come or even where they disappeared to.

After it was all over, Cleary realized he'd never even drawn his gun from its holster, yet Moody had single-handedly managed to kill one man and send the other two scuttling while keeping hold of the pack animal. Embarrassed by his lack of preparedness, he vowed to be more observant and on-guard.

"You can't be a passenger on that horse, Daniel," was all Moody said when the melee was over.

"Yes, sir," Cleary meekly answered. "It won't happen again."

After they'd pitched camp that night, Cleary finally asked, "How did you know they were coming, Richard?"

"You never know, kid. You assume they will, and you wait for them. Keep an eye on likely places where you can be attacked. Keep an eye ahead *and* behind. This isn't a bird-watching outing."

Cleary nodded and remained silent.

"One of the things Mexicans are real keen on is horse flesh. Can't just tie up the horses for the night unless you're truly in the middle of nowhere. We're still close to Tijuana and a few settlements. They know we're here," Moody explained. "So from here on out, the fires are extinguished after we eat, if we have a fire at all, and the horses are literally brought in close. Close enough you can feel their breath."

"What about keeping guard?"

"If that's what you want, but I guarantee you won't hear them coming. If there were more of us, I'd say okay, but with only the two of us, we might as well sleep – sleep might be hard to come by soon enough," Moody said, throwing dirt onto the small campfire. "Now, try and get some rest."

Despite his fear, Cleary fell asleep almost instantly. He awoke several times during the night, however, and each time saw Moody with a rifle in his hands. *What have I gotten into?* he wondered.

The aroma of coffee and the smell of smoke awakened the young marshal. He felt almost joyous to have survived the night.

"We've got a long day ahead of us," Moody said as he finished loading the pack horse. "Grab some coffee and a biscuit and let's make tracks." Without any argument, Cleary did as told and within a half an hour the two men rode out.

They made good time and stopped in La Mision late that afternoon. "We should make Ensenada by tomorrow evening. We'll bypass the town, though," Moody said, "and head southeast for about two weeks. Maybe three. Depends on the heat – and the bandidos – I suppose."

"How is it you're so familiar with this area?" Cleary asked, dismounting.

"Let's just say Jake and I spent a great deal of time down here."

"That's when you two went on that rescue mission for the kidnapped women?" Cleary asked.

Moody nodded. "Listen, I'm going to try and barter with that senora over there and see if for a few pesos I can get us a meal and a place to sleep."

"Isn't that risky? What if our horses get stolen?" Cleary asked, highly concerned.

"We should be okay here," Moody said. "I've seen a couple of men who look like they're here on behalf of Fuentes. If they're going to follow us to San Felipe, our troubles are over."

Cleary quickly looked around. Then he saw them – two men draped in heavy gun belts crisscrossing their chests lounging on the opposite side of the street. "You sure they're Diego Fuentes' men?"

"Count on it. Look at the other people around here, then take a good gander at those men. They don't live here, Daniel. They're what you'd call *militars.* Fuentes' soldiers. Go ahead and stare."

Daniel's heart skipped a beat when he furtively studied the two ferocious-looking men on the opposite corner. From their high leather boots to the full sombreros and bushy mustaches, the men indeed looked out of place in the tiny two-street stop in the middle of nowhere. "They got gun belts around their waists *and* across their chests," Daniel exclaimed.

"They're called bandoliers," Moody answered. "Convenient and certainly handy."

"Maybe we should get some," Daniel commented.

In the morning Fuentes' two *militars* watched Moody and Cleary saddle up and load the pack horse. No sooner had they mounted, however, than the *militars* fetched their own horses. At first the Mexicans followed at a respectful distance, but as the morning passed, they drew closer. Every time Cleary turned in his saddle hoping to see the men gone, they remained in sight.

"No point in worrying about them, Daniel," Moody counseled. "They're not here to kill us. Diego will want to do that. They're here to make sure no one else kills us."

"Somehow that doesn't really make me feel better," Daniel said.

"It's better, at least for now. We won't be robbed, either," Moody added.

"What did you mean, 'at least for now'?" Cleary asked a few moments later. "Will it get dangerous later?"

"Of course. They won't take kindly to my killing them."

"Huh! When do you plan on doing that?"

"There's a pass about a week or so from here. It'll be a good place where we might be able to ride ahead and then circle behind them. I'll kill them then. Or maybe once we reach the gulf. Haven't really decided yet. I'll let you know. Maybe you can be of help, you think?"

Daniel nodded determinedly, Moody's swagger and contagious confidence having a good effect on the young marshal.

Even Moody seemed surprised, however, when the two *militars* rode into their campsite that evening and joined them. No one spoke. Moody looked the men over. Daniel finally summoned the courage to do likewise. He noticed the Mexicans seemed to have better provisions, and they ate in silence without acknowledging the them.

"They going to be with us like this the rest of the way?" Daniel spoke in a low voice.

"They think they are," Moody replied, his back to the men. "Think of them as an armed escort. Listen, Daniel, they're not here to kill us. Relax. We'll get our chance. They'll grow careless when they get drunk."

"When will that happen?"

"When I bring out the bottles of tequila I bought at our last stop," Moody replied, smiling slyly. "I'll wait until we head due south. There won't be many banditos along the coastal road. Too many poor people to bother with."

"So we're not doing the circling back and coming up behind them, then?"

"Not when they're apparently going to travel with us all the way. Change of plans."

"I'm glad you're here, Moody. Never thought I'd ever say anything like that," Daniel said, worry written on his face.

Ben McGraw could not be found. No matter how badly Fernando and Raphael beat McGraw's woman, she swore she did not know where her man had gone. With swollen lips, busted teeth, puffy eyes, and hair ripped from her head, she tried to explain that he often disappeared for days at a time – on business, she claimed. The last ferocious punch to the side of her head killed Consuela Jiminez. Livid at the woman's refusal to tell them what they wanted to know, and frightened at having to face Fuentes without McGraw in custody, the men pummeled and kicked Consuela's limp body until it lay completely broken. Then they set fire to the small hacienda. As they watched the flames loudly crackle and ignite the tinder-dry, palm-bough roof, Fernando slumped forward. At first Raphael thought his companion was fighting pangs of guilt for the wrong they did the woman which had sickened even him, but then Raphael felt a burning in his neck. His eyes remained opened as he toppled from his horse, helpless to move. He landed on the ground, feeling nothing from the fall but a stinging sensation in his neck. Through fading vision he saw a gringo standing over him, pointing a pistol at his head. Blackness followed.

McGraw stood over the dead man a moment, then pulled an unresponsive Fernando from the saddle. "Thanks, gentlemen, I can get good money for these horses." He spat on both men before leading the two animals away. He could feel the heat from his burning house. It was over. He could not stay in Mexico. Diego Fuentes would know who killed his men. It didn't matter that the men had killed an innocent woman. Fuentes only cared about his *militas.*

I just made things a helluva lot easier for Richard Moody, McGraw thought as he mounted his horse. *Now he has two less men to deal with.*

McGraw could never return to San Felipe. He'd have to move on. His best choice was to ride south toward Puertocito, a small fishing village. Possibly he could stay there for a few days and try to hire a Mexican to ferry him across the gulf to mainland Mexico. He'd use the horses as payment. If there were no boats capable of transporting him that distance across the often rough sea, he'd be forced to continue on to a bigger port that was at least a two-week ride south. The problem with going further, he knew with certainty, was that he'd have to travel inland to access roads. The coastal road ended a few miles past Puertocito. He'd be easy pickings for bandits or any of Fuentes' roving *militas* if he headed further south.

Despite his clear, logical thinking, McGraw found himself riding north toward San Felipe. Could he ride through town unnoticed? It'd be much easier getting out of Mexico by riding north and then heading toward Ensenada – if he could make it by San Felipe. Having ridden down from that area, he remembered the road as well-traveled with several small missions and settlements in all but the most mountainous, hazardous parts.

He cursed as he continued northward, knowing himself to be a fool for heading into the wilderness with no water, no supplies, and only enough cartridges to hold off a few men for a short time. Despite all this, he felt he had no choice but to continue on. Traveling south would never work.

Diego Fuentes grew moodier and more pensive as each day passed. The big man could admit to no one but himself that he no longer enjoyed forays into his territory like he used to. He disliked being away from his spacious hacienda in Guerrero Negro. "I am getting to be an old man," he said in a low voice as he finished a bottle of tequila. He tried to remember his age but could not. He knew he had to be around 50-years-old, probably older since he remembered thinking he was around 50 a few years ago. "I am too old to be chasing around for the simple pleasure of revenge," he murmured.

A strong urge to return to Guerrero Negro swept over him. He asked himself why he cared so much about killing Richard Moody. It wasn't about the woman he and the gunman both loved and lost. In Diego's mind women were a commodity to be used and discarded. Margarita had been special, but even her specialness would have faded in time. No, it was about being duped and made a fool of. Moody had no respect – that was the problem. Jake Silver respected him. Moody had no sense of decorum. In Diego's world, decorum and respect meant everything.

"I must kill Moody, then I am finished." Smart enough to see that Americanos held too much power, Diego had a foreboding that his era of rule would end soon. Younger, and yes, bolder men would have to struggle with the Americanos and the growth of young Mexican upstarts who also did not know anything of decorum and respect. But despite his reluctance to stay, Diego could not bring himself to return home until he saw Moody's body left as carrion for wild dogs and coyotes.

"Shouldn't you have heard from that friend of yours by now?" Virginia Hall asked as she took her place at the table.

Jake Silver smiled. Virginia almost never referred to Richard Moody by name – always as that friend, or acquaintance, or even *that man*. "Yes, I'm a bit surprised considering I suggested the two return if nothing came up within a few days of their investigation," Jake agreed.

"Well, as I recall, that friend of yours rather does as he pleases," Virginia said, a note of disapproval in her voice. "I'm far more concerned about Daniel, however," she added in a softer tone.

"Daniel will be okay with Richard. They're onto something, I'm sure, or they'd have returned."

"What if they're dead somewhere, Jake? Have you thought of that? How can you be so sure they're alright?"

Jake looked at the older woman for a moment. "You're right, Virginia," he finally said. "Something could have happened, but I know Richard, and I have confidence in the man to stay alive. Now, let's change the subject. Little pitchers have big ears."

"Well, you'd think he could send a telegram at the very least," Virginia said, a note of finality in her voice.

Jake reached over to help Maggie cut her small piece of meat and did not respond. In truth, he *was* worried about Richard and Daniel. He feared, even suspected, the two had crossed into Mexico in pursuit of Baker and McKinney. He'd sent a telegram to Yuma inquiring of the local law enforcement if Moody had passed through. The response was that the two lawmen had gone toward San Diego.

Had Moody crossed the border, Jake would have been compelled to follow, knowing that the long arm of Diego Fuentes might well entrap his friend. But San Diego?

10

"Lookee here, Buddy! You're in the paper," Ansel Axelsen announced, amazement on the old man's face.

Puzzled, thirteen-year-old Buddy Reed looked up from the barrel of line he'd been coiling. "What'cha mean, Ansel?"

"Right here. Says it on this page," the old fisherman replied as he took his finger to slowly trace the words. "It says 'Buddy Reed. See Campbell at 183 Dawson Street, San Diego.'"

Buddy finished coiling the fishing line then stepped into the boat's small cabin. "Let me see."

"Right there. Either you're a wanted man, or a lucky man. No tellin'," Ansel said. "Don't know if in all my years I've ever known anyone who had a notice in the paper with their name on it and all. Unless it was a 'Wanted' notice." Ansel laughed.

"Should I go? Do you think there might be another Buddy Reed?"

"Yah. Likely there's a few more Buddy Reeds out there, I reckon."

Buddy looked at the notice for several minutes. "It must be another Buddy Reed. I don't know anyone who would post a notice in a newspaper for me."

Ansel slowly nodded. "Might it be your mother?"

Buddy shrugged. He'd all but given up hope of ever finding his mother. She'd up and left after he ran off to work on a ranch. Didn't tell anyone where she was going either. He'd searched for her for better than a year, but it had been a waste of time.

"If ya want, I can go with ya. Back ya up," Ansel offered. "I think ya best go, lad. Might be good news. And if it's a different Buddy they're a lookin' for, well, it's no matter."

Buddy stood silent for a moment, considering Ansel's advice. "Yeah. You're probably right, Ansel. It's probably someone else. Another Buddy Reed." He paused, a troubled look passing over his face. "Maybe I'll go. Maybe I won't. We got good weather now for fishing. I'll go after our next trip out…if the notice is still in the paper."

Ansel nodded and watched the shaggy-haired, wiry teenager return to the deck to coil line and bait hooks.

Despite his seeming disinterest, Buddy couldn't stop thinking about the notice in the paper. What if it was his mother trying to contact him? Somehow he doubted that was the case. Besides, he knew he'd changed over the past few years. Despite his age, he wasn't a little boy anymore. Likely his mother would want to swoop in and make him dress like a dandy and go back to school.

A shadow passed over him and he looked up. "What is it, Ansel?"

"I can see by your face, Buddy, that somethin's troublin' you. Ya want to talk about it, maybe?"

Buddy shrugged. "Not much to talk about, Ansel. I was just wonderin' if it was my mom, you know. It'd be good to know she's alive and okay, but after all these years I – I'm different. I don't want to change my life. I like it here on the boat with you. I like fishing. Someday I want to have my very own boat. You know that."

"Someday, Buddy, this boat will be yours," Ansel replied. "You can support an old man then."

"No, I'll hire you," the boy said, an engaging smile on his tanned face.

"Tell you what, Buddy. Let's you and me go to this here address and find out what this is all about. That way you'll know once and for all and it won't pester you none."

Buddy smiled. "Okay. You go with me."

"Put your work aside and put on a clean shirt. In fact, we should clean up and look respectable. I ought to take a pair of scissors to that wild stuff you got growing on your head while we're scrubbing up," Ansel said, looking at the boy's sun-bleached mop of hair.

"I'm not willing to go to all that trouble," Buddy said. "Don't get carried away! Let's just go."

"No, lad. We got to get the fish scales off at the very least."

The harbor master drew a map showing them how to get to the address listed in the paper, and the two set off for Dawson Street that afternoon. It would be a long walk unless they splurged and took a newfangled streetcar. "Let's take that streetcar yonder," suggested Ansel, his old legs already weary. "We can take our time when we walk back."

George Campbell watched two unlikely customers approach the swanky entry to his bank. A boy and an old man walked cautiously through the doors and looked around, wide-eyed and nervous. Both looked downtrodden to Campbell, but that's the way many of his customers looked in San Diego. The people out West were a motely lot and nothing like his previous, well-heeled Eastern customers.

Campbell nodded to his assistant who occupied a desk to his left, and the young man approached the two intruders.

"May I help you?" he asked.

Ansel spoke up when Buddy remained uncharacteristically silent. "Yes you may, young man. We're here on business with a man named Campbell. I'd be obliged if you'd point him out to us."

"Do you have an appointment?"

"This here's our appointment," Ansel replied, showing the tattered page with personal ads.

"I see. And which of you is Buddy Reed?"

Ansel motioned toward Buddy.

"Just one moment, please."

Buddy and Ansel watched the young man approach a much older, distinguished-looking gentleman sitting behind a monstrous desk. The two men spoke quietly for a few moments, and then the young one returned.

"Please follow me."

Buddy noted the banker hesitate before shaking Ansel's hand. "Please, be seated," the man said. "I'm George Campbell. And you are?"

"Name's Ansel Axelsen. This here's Buddy Reed. We found this notice in the paper today," Ansel said, sliding the rumpled page across Campbell's desk.

Campbell looked down at the ad, then at the two seated across from him. "Yes. This ad has been running for several weeks."

"Well, we been fishin'," Ansel explained.

Campbell turned to Buddy. "So, you're Buddy Reed," he stated, more than asked. Not waiting for an answer, he said, "Tell me about yourself."

"What's to tell? I'm fishing now with Ansel, and I plan on bein' a fisherman," Buddy replied.

"Buddy," Campbell began, "you will need to tell me something of your background to convince me that you are who you say you are."

"Excuse me, feller, but what's this all about, if you don't mind my askin'?"

"A gentleman who will remain unnamed for now, or at least until Buddy speaks of him, came into this establishment a few weeks ago. He left strict instructions that if a boy named Buddy Reed should respond to this ad, the boy was to prove his identity in some way," Campbell patiently explained. "Once I'm convinced of the boy's identity, that is to say it's been proven to my satisfaction, I have been instructed to give the boy a sum of money. The rest of the funds are to be wired to a bank in Prescott, Arizona, and will be dispersed to Buddy as needed by a person there whom Buddy must also be able to tell about," Campbell paused. "That is all I am able to reveal to you until I am convinced of this boy's identity."

All three sat in silence for a moment. Finally Buddy said, "Well, I don't know what you want to know, but I was born up on the Rim in Arizona."

"What 'rim' would that be?" Campbell asked, withdrawing a slim folder from a drawer.

"I think it was called something like the Muggy Rim, or something like that. My ma and I left there after my dad was killed." Buddy stopped, not sure what to say next. "We had a small ranch."

"And where did you go when you left the rim?" Campbell asked, in an effort to help.

"We went to Prescott with Marshal Jake Silver and my uncle Richard," Buddy replied. "And a girl was there that my uncle was kind of sweet on, I think."

"And?" Campbell said trying to encourage the boy.

"Well, as best I recollect me and my ma lived in Phoenix for a spell, then we moved to San Diego. She…she wanted to send me to some fancy school in Missouri or somewhere like that, but I didn't want to go, so I ran away and got a job on a ranch," Buddy's voice grew shaky. "After a bit I got to missin' my mom and so I left, but this time when I come on back home my mom wasn't there no more. I can't find her."

Campbell leaned back in his chair, his face relaxed as he studied Buddy. A frown creased his brow, however, when his gaze moved to Ansel Axelsen. "Mr. Axelsen, what is your interest in this young man, if you don't mind my asking?"

Ansel's expression said that he knew what the line of questioning was really about. "Well, Mr. Campbell, Buddy here works with me on my boat, *Queen Fisher*. We fish for cod, jack, shark sometimes, and some tuna. Pretty much anything that swims, actually."

"How long has Buddy been doing this?"

Ansel turned to Buddy, "How long you been with me, son?"

"Close to two years," Buddy replied. "Remember, you hired me right after you broke your wrist."

"Ah, yes. I remember now. The lad says two years, so two years it is," Ansel stated.

"You understand, Mr. Axelsen, that the money involved is strictly for Buddy. He'll be given a travel allowance to Prescott," Campbell explained. "Once there, he will be under the guardianship of U.S. Marshal Jake Silver until which time that Mr. Moody, his uncle, returns from business in Mexico."

"That is perfectly clear and as it should be," Ansel replied, his voice growing tense. "I'm not a freeloader or an abuser, Mr. Campbell. I don't take kindly to your inference."

"No insult intended, Mr. Axelsen. This is just a very complicated – shall we say – an extremely complicated and risky situation. My reputation is at stake. Mr. Moody was most exacting in his demands."

"I don't want to go to Prescott," Buddy blurted. "I want to be a fisherman like Ansel. I won't go!"

Silence descended on the trio. Campbell's eyebrows shifted up and down and his fingers drummed nervously on the desk. It was obvious to all present that the man had not expected a refusal. Finally, Mr. Campbell spoke. "Buddy, you have little choice in this matter. You are a juvenile. Your mother has died. Your uncle appears to be your only living kin. He is your legal guardian."

"My mother's dead?" Buddy asked, his face crestfallen.

"I'm sorry to have to be the one to tell you. She died in Arizona. I don't know the details, but your uncle informed me of this when he was making these arrangements."

Buddy sat, his face a portrait of anguish. Only Ansel knew that Buddy lived, and often talked, in continuous hope that his mother was alive and would return. "I still don't want to go to Prescott," he murmured.

"Very well. I'll inform your uncle when he returns. It's not my intention to inform authorities, not that anyone would do a thing about it," Campbell said. "May I again inquire the name of your vessel, Mr. Axelsen? I'm quite certain Mr. Moody will at least want to see Buddy."

"*Queen Fisher* is the boat's name," Ansel snapped.

"Yes, yes, I remember now. *Queen Fisher,"* he said as he wrote the name on a piece of paper in the folder.

"Since you do not intend to cooperate at this time, I have been instructed to give you $500 for your use as you see fit. However, I assure you that Mr. Moody will be most perturbed about your refusal to relocate to Prescott, Buddy. Please think this over. Should you change your mind, you may return at any time and we will proceed with the disbursement of your funds." Campbell stood as he finished speaking, letting Ansel and Buddy know their time was up. "My assistant will withdraw $500 from the account for you. Follow him to the counter."

Stunned about the news of his mother's death, the money, and the option to move to Prescott, Buddy simply stood and nodded.

Once outside the bank with the $500 in his pocket, Buddy and Ansel began the long trek back to the boat. Dumbfounded by what Campbell had told them, the two walked in silence, not noticing he distance.

As they neared the wharf, Ansel finally said, "Maybe you should reconsider all this, Buddy. Sleep on it for a day or two. You might be better off in Prescott. Fishing is dangerous business, as you well know." The old man's shoulders sagged as the two walked along. "My life has near passed me by. You've got an opportunity, Buddy, to be someone. Sounds like your uncle has lots of money and just about anything is possible for you. You don't want to end up a broken old man like me, son." Ansel waited for Buddy's response, and when none came he continued. "I know you think you're beholden to me for giving you a job and taking you off the streets. But you done me a lot of good, young man. You saved my life too, you know. You made it possible for me to keep doin' what I love best. And maybe it's time I put the *Queen Fisher* up for sale and moved ashore."

"I'm stayin' with you, Ansel. I don't want to talk about this anymore."

Buddy's fishing line, what Ansel called a meat-hook, that he'd draped over the side of the boat had a nice snapper on it, so the two ate fish and the vegetables they'd bought with a small bit of Buddy's new-found money.

"I guess I best write Marshal Silver a letter," Buddy said after the two had gone to their bunks for the night. "Tell him I'm not coming."

"That's a fine idea, Buddy. A fine idea," Ansel said, hoping that perhaps the boy would have a change of heart.

"I'll write it in the morning and take it to the post before we leave. That okay with you, Ansel?"

"Fine idea, Buddy. That way no one will get worried and stir up more trouble for you."

"What kind of trouble?"

"Well…like comin' over here to take you back. You know how them lawmen can get. Mighty determined."

"Okay. I'll write. I'll tell him I'm 16 now. I don't think he'll remember how old I was when he last saw me," Buddy said, recalling Jake Silver. "I really liked Marshal Silver. I think he liked my mom and me too. He stayed with us a long time, you know, helping us out and all. I was kinda hoping ma would marry him. But I guess she didn't like him as much as I did. I'll write him first thing in the morning."

"That's good thinking. A fine idea."

11

Jake Silver stared out the train window and marveled at the magnificent, orange moon that filled the eastern horizon as it made its ascent. Momentarily his worries faded. He remembered the many nights he'd been on the trail when the moon rose, transforming the desert into a place of indescribable beauty. All that was before, though. Before Betsy died.

He still struggled with the decision he'd made to leave Maggie and Henry for this fool's errand. He knew that the old housekeeper, Virginia, and the ranch hand Thomas would take good care of the children. Still, his leave-taking had been painful for both Maggie and him. Should the worst befall him and he didn't survive, his sister Sophie and her husband would care for the children – probably far better than he could.

"Promise you'll come back, Daddy! Promise!" Maggie had sobbed when he'd left the ranch. How could he promise? God knew he wanted to return. He didn't want to leave, but he couldn't stop himself.

He withdrew Buddy Reed's letter from his pocket and read it again.

**

To Marshal Silver:

Dear Marshal Silver, I hope you remember me. You came to my ma's ranch some years back and took us to Prescut. Then my mom and me went on to Phenix. Then we came to Californya. Anyway, I'm writin to tell you that I'm not comin back to Prescut. My uncle Richard wants me to go to Prescut until he gets back from Mexico. I got my own life now, Marshal Silver. I'm grown up now and I don't need no one watchin out for me. I hope you understand. I also herd my mom died. I don't know how or when or where cuz I was working on a ranch. But she is gone now and I am taking care of myself. I don't mean no disrespect. You were a good man to us. I will see uncle Richard when he comes back I gess.

Buddy Reed

**

Jake carefully folded the missive and put it in a leather wallet he kept in a pocket inside his vest.

Mexico. What the hell was Richard doing in Mexico? And Daniel had to be with him since the young deputy marshal hadn't returned. Jake's thoughts of Mexico and the time he'd spent there both attracted him and repelled him. Ever since he'd heard that Ben McGraw had taken up residence in San Felipe, he'd planned on returning at some distant date when Maggie was a grown woman. By that time he'd have savored the idea of revenge to such a degree that he wouldn't care if he lived or not. And he suspected there'd be a showdown with Diego Fuentes and his army of bandits thrown into the mix at that time, too. Somehow word traveled like wildfire in that godforsaken land. Fuentes knew what people were going to do before they even knew what they were going to do. Still, he had to return. He couldn't count on being lucky this time around, though. He'd had enough luck to last a lifetime when he'd been saved by Fuentes and then kept a prisoner for months – a "house guest" as Fuentes often referred to his captivity. Jake's escape from Fuentes had been nothing short of miraculous. Richard Moody had risked all to return for him – now he had to do the same for Richard.

After checking with several law enforcement folks along the border, the information that found its way over the border indicated that Fuentes was in San Felipe, and that Richard and Daniel were on their way there. Jake could not begin to understand why Moody would venture south of the border in pursuit of Baker and McKinney. They were bad, murderous men, but not worth the risk Moody was taking. Something else had to be going on. The fact that Moody and Cleary had no jurisdiction whatsoever in Mexico also lent a degree of mystery and urgency to Jake's decision to leave Prescott and find the two men.

"You are not the marshal in Mexico," Virginia had argued. "You can't go down there and mete out justice, Jake."

"My badge is on my desk, Virginia," Jake had said. His look silenced the motherly, old woman and kept her from arguing further.

Jake had made arrangements to disembark the train at Gila Bend. From there it would be at least a two-day ride to the border town of Sonoita where he planned on paying Juan Robles, a Mexican who catered to the few Americans who traveled to that area, to accompany him on the rip to Puerto Penasco, a tiny fishing village consisting of a couple dozen palapa huts. From there Juan would arrange for his cousin, a fisherman, to take him to San Felipe via boat. It would not be easy to cross the gulf, but it was doable if conditions didn't become too rough.

Jake didn't know how long Moody and Cleary had been traveling in Mexico, but he did know that if it were true that they were riding overland, as he'd heard, they'd be on the trail for several weeks at the very least. He hoped he would arrive in San Felipe before them.

After the train made its pre-arranged stop, Jake retrieved his horse and pack-horse from the livestock car, waved to the conductor, then turned south as the locomotive chugged slowly down the tracks, bound for Yuma and then on to San Diego.

Although it had grown dark, the full moon made travel easy and certainly less scorching than travel in the blazing mid-day heat. In the distance he saw a dim light, probably from the home of a hardy soul trying to establish himself in the vast, arid desert. Jake remembered the area well. He'd rescued his sister who'd ended up in dire straits there, kidnapped by an Apache.[8] Not far from where he now rode he'd had encounters with the Indian, Nantan Lupan. The Indian and Jake had become fast friends in the end, and the Apache had a way of always showing up when help was needed the most, but Jake knew better than to count on the Apache this time.

Finding a well-worn trail, Jake made good time. He felt exuberant despite a sense of dread lurking in the background. He thoroughly enjoyed being back on the trail instead of sitting behind a desk. The isolation and the silence of the land around him felt magnificent and lulled him into a sense of harmony with the desert. The howls of coyotes reminded him he was no stranger to a life in the open. Many a night he'd enjoyed the comfort of a small fire to cook a meal by, and the warmth of the sunbaked desert for a resting place. Despite his errand of death, Jake felt at peace for the first time since Betsy's death. He realized he didn't belong behind a desk. He'd known it all along, but for the sake of his daughter he'd settled in. Now he wasn't so sure he could go back. Maybe he wouldn't have to. Maybe it would finally end for him in San Felipe. He tried not to think of Maggie and Henry. He knew they'd be well-cared for by his sister and her husband if anything happened to him, though. Maggie would never want for anything. Maybe it would be better this way.

---

[8] *Apache Book II*

Ben McGraw skirted San Felipe in the dark, but he stopped at two small huts far off the traveled passageway. At both huts he bartered for what he needed, giving a horse for payment. The unsuspecting, poor farmers were thrilled with the trade, unaware that the horses belonged to Diego Fuentes and that possessing them would mean certain death.

Once McGraw had made what he considered sufficient tracks northwest so that he could halt and rest without fear of capture, he stopped. After unsaddling and hobbling his animal, he tried to doze, but anxiety and fear gnawed at him too much. He knew his mount needed rest, however, so he forced himself to linger.

So far, he'd thought of nothing on the trip but escape. Now that escape actually seemed possible, he realized he had no idea of his destination. He remembered Jarvis McKinney talking about California and thought that might be where he'd head. It was populated enough that a stranger riding into any town wouldn't be looked upon with suspicion, what with miners and ranchers pouring into the area, and he'd heard it was possible to ride north into Oregon if needed.

Having a destination in mind calmed him somewhat. But he knew he had a hell of a long way to go before he'd be out of Mexico and Fuentes' long reach. Dare he travel on established routes? Traveling alone across country with limited supplies could be deadly. He'd have to take his chances, he supposed, and stick to the main route. He might have a good two or three-day head-start before Fuentes learned of the deaths of his men. In two or three days he could be perhaps sixty or more miles away if his horse didn't go lame. If the horse went lame, it'd be all over.

With his thoughts on the future, McGraw began to relax. Soon he slept.

The sun had risen when McGraw awoke with a start. Anxiously he looked about. He finally spied his horse by a clump of ocotillo bushes, stripping the dried leaves from the thorny plants.

Once saddled, McGraw debated traveling east a bit to pick up the easy gulf road. He'd heard the direct route north could be marshy, with quicksand and other hazards. That route would get him out of Mexico faster, *if* he made it. He had a good day's ride before he had to make the final decision whether to head north or turn west toward Ensenada. One look at the distant looming black sky, however, convinced him that the better, although longer, choice was to head west. A heavy rain would make the marsh areas impassable.

Once mounted, McGraw made a snap decision to travel northwest instead by cutting cross-country. Maybe he could lop some miles off his journey. He'd completely bypass the junction where the gulf road met the route to Ensenada. If he looked hard enough, he could just make out a trail made by others trying to cut the journey to Ensenada shorter which he hoped just might also make his passage shorter, although he suspected he'd encounter steep, rough terrain. Still, if he could avoid bandits and Fuentes' men it would be worth the trouble.

It didn't take long for McGraw to grow frustrated. At times the trail completely petered out, only to be clearly visible two hundred yards later. He questioned whether men had traveled this route or just wild animals. In any event, it would still cut distance off his journey. He felt cooked by the mid-day heat but nothing in the godforsaken country offered any shade. The going was slow and he began to regret his earlier decision. For a spell he contemplated turning back and just starting all over by heading north into the marsh. Then he wondered if staying to the gulf road might not have been better. Every idea seemed better than the last, but still he doggedly kept going.

Judging by the sun, it was late afternoon when McGraw espied what looked to be a small group of travelers on the main road from Ensenada. Something about the assemblage of the group troubled him. Retrieving a spyglass from his saddlebag, he thought he could make out two American-looking riders in front. There was, however, no mistaking the heavily-armed Mexicans who rode behind, their large sombreros and visible bandoliers giving them away.

Puzzled by the procession, McGraw sat and watched for a spell as the group moved slowly along. Obscured by the rocky terrain, he took his time looking through the spyglass trying to decipher whether the travelers would be friend or foe.

"I'll be damned. Is that you, Richard Moody?" McGraw spoke in a low voice. "I'll be damned," he repeated. "My lucky day, you son of a bitch. You stood trial for that murdering wench, and now I'll hang you for perjury since the jury wouldn't."

Still McGraw remained on the hillside transfixed by the scene. He was not so anxious for revenge that he was willing to ride into a couple of armed Mexicans and Moody, a fast draw at close range. He watched the group halt. It looked as though the Mexicans, with their arms and hands waving about, were doing all the talking. After a few minutes of what appeared to be heated discussion, the bandits motioned for the other two travelers to follow them. McGraw watched the group make camp a quarter-mile off the road.

Driven by hatred for Moody's part in the death of his son, McGraw worked his way slowly down the steep, rocky terrain, making sure to remain out of view of the other travelers. It would be difficult to take all four on, but all he needed was one good shot to Moody's head. Just one, then he could die a happy man.

He angled his horse toward a cactus-covered hillock. He'd stay put until dusk, then he'd close in. If luck was with him, he'd get all four of them along with a lot of cartridges and supplies.

Richard Moody kept a close eye on the Mexican bandits accompanying him and Cleary. He kept a watch on Cleary also, who was growing increasingly nervous and agitated as the days passed. In Moody's estimation, the Mexicans would not be a problem, but he worried that Cleary would unravel.

"Daniel, if you want to live through this, you have to relax," he said for the umpteenth time. It had become a ritual – reassuring the kid that things would work out.

Daniel gave a scornful laugh. "That's easy for you to say, Moody. It's driving me crazy not knowing what these guys are rattling on about. Plus it's damn hot and…well, hot."

"Kid, if you're going to stay in Arizona, you better learn the language spoken down here. I have a feeling you'll need to know it more than you realize."

"Doesn't that constant, loud babble drive you crazy?"

"Not so much. Again, think of it this way, Daniel, as long as these guys are with us, we won't be robbed or attacked. Think of them as an armed escort."

"That's hard to do, and you know it," Daniel replied, tossing a few small cactus ribs onto the fire. "How did you and Jake manage all those months you were here?"

"Hell, Jake speaks that language like he's one of them. I'd say he's totally fluent in it."

"Huh! I didn't know that," Daniel said, a surprised look on his face. "Maybe he could teach me some. Plus, I'm nervous 'cause I don't know when anything is going to happen."

"I'll give you plenty of warning, I assure you. I'm thinking we'll see the gulf in about a day. We'll kill them then."

"Richard, I – I've never killed anyone before."

"Trust me on this: when it's either your life or theirs, it's easy. The important thing is to not let one of them escape. Shoot for the head if possible," Moody advised. "If you don't have a good head shot, a shot to the chest gets the job done too. Just don't go wounding one of them. Pump them full of bullets until they don't twitch anymore. We can't have one of them escaping, Daniel."

"You make it sound so easy."

"It is. Get use to it or turn in your badge when we get back."

After a few minutes Daniel asked, "Hey, how do you know we're only a day from the gulf?"

"Can't you smell it?" Moody asked, showing a rare smile. "Smell the air very carefully, and you'll smell water."

Daniel sat for several minutes staring into the fire and breathing deeply, and Moody detected the young man's facial muscles begin to relax. "Hey, Richard. I think you're full of shit. I don't smell anything except smoke. And, I been meaning to ask, I noticed you kept looking at something in the distance earlier today. What'd you see?"

"I'm not positive, but I think I saw a lone rider up on the ridge just south of us a bit. My eyes aren't the best though. Tomorrow take a few looks, but don't make it obvious. Don't let the Mexicans see you."

"What if it's one of them?"

"I don't think it is or the rider would've advanced. Could just be someone on another trail. But once I thought I saw a gleam, like maybe the sun reflecting off a spyglass. I've never seen a Mexican use a spyglass – leastwise not these kinds of Mexicans."

"Could it be help? Maybe someone keeping an eye on us and waiting to attack?"

Richard thought about Daniel's suggestions for several minutes. Finally he said, "No. I don't think so. If I could see better I'd know for certain, though."

12

Under cover of dark, Ben McGraw left his horse secured to a downed mesquite tree a half a mile from Moody's campsite and took off on foot, carrying his canteen, rifle and a pouch of cartridges. Excitement buoyed him and he had to remind himself to walk slowly and cautiously. Any unusual noise could alert the other horses who would signal the four men that something was astir.

McGraw did not approach the camp directly, but circled around, looking for the best position from which to shoot – and then escape. It took better than two hours of cautiously creeping about to find the location that perfectly suited him. Soaked with perspiration, he drank heavily from the canteen and sat behind a large boulder for a bit to collect himself. The moon was nearly full, so vision would be good. The shot would be nothing compared to the bullet he'd fired into Betsy McGraw's head. Now that had been a shot for the record books.

After daring to cautiously stand and lean against the boulder, McGraw studied Moody's campsite. Slowly he returned to a sitting position, his back against the warm granite. He'd have to wait until things quieted down. There was too much commotion around the campsite to shoot. He wondered who the young man was traveling with Moody. He didn't think it was Moody's son, for the boy was taller and bigger than the gunman, and he had a head of dark hair also. McGraw remembered Moody as being scrawny and blond.

McGraw sighed and looked up at the stars. He was not a religious man, although he use to attend church with his wife – before she left him. That was another sore spot caused by his ex-daughter-in-law. He'd told his son Gunner not to marry the girl, that she didn't love him. Gunner, however, was so smitten with that vixen he turned deaf to all counsel and advice. Sure enough, she no sooner married Gunner than Jake Silver returned. It didn't take but a moment before that slip of a girl began cavorting with the marshal. Gunner should have seen through her when she started batting those blue eyes at him. McGraw suspected the truth of the matter was that Betsy had gotten with child yet again by Silver, and with him gone who knows where, she grabbed the first available man to cast some legitimacy on her bastard child. A second one, no less.

McGraw wiped the sweat from his face and shook the nearly empty canteen. He had to save what little water he had for the fast trip back to his horse. He grew agitated and fidgeted with his rifle as he remembered Betsy slumping into Jake Silver's arms after the bullet entered her beautiful head. *Too bad her little girl saw it,* he thought as he recalled the scene. Then he chided himself for taking pity on any person associated at all with Betsy.

In an effort to shake the memory of the crying child, McGraw tried to remember Gunner as the young man lie in his casket. Betsy'd emptied a revolver into his son's mid-section after Gunner, in a rage, back-shot Jake Silver. Problem was, Jake didn't die. Gunner did, and the little wench never stood trial. Richard Moody claimed he'd shot Gunner. Not a person in Prescott believed that cockamamie story, but the smooth-tongued Moody had the jury eating out of his hand, and a not-guilty verdict came quickly.

The more McGraw tried not to think about what happened, the angrier he grew until his heartbeat thundered in his ears. "Gotta even the score," he muttered. "Moody kept me from getting justice." Killing Betsy had not brought him the satisfaction he'd hoped it would.

Slowly McGraw stood and studied the scene, his legs shaky. The men seemed to have settled in for the evening, and the campfire, though low, still burned bright enough for him to take a shot. Moody and the boy sat facing him, the fire clearly illuminating them. The Mexicans had their backs to him. McGraw rested his arm on the rock and slowly positioned his rifle and leaned in.

"So, you think tomorrow is going to be the day you kill, I mean, *we* kill them two?" Daniel asked in a low undertone.

Moody sat quite still before he answered. "Maybe it'll be tonight."

"Tonight?" Cleary asked, clearly shocked.

"I got a bad feeling, Daniel. A real bad feeling."

"A feeling about what? You getting sick? You some kind of fortune teller or something?"

"Kid, you better learn to pay attention to your intuition. It's like a sixth sense. Don't write things off."

"Moody, you are really making me more than a bit edgy. What in Sam Hill is going on with you?" Daniel asked, his voice growing tense.

"Someone's out there," Moody said.

Daniel looked about. "Where? Out there in the dark?"

Moody nodded.

"How do you know that? I don't see, or hear, a dang thing."

"*You* might not, but watch the horses."

Daniel studied the four horses for a bit. "Well, I just see 'em standing there looking around. They're not raising a fuss."

"They're nervous, Daniel. Not relaxed. The ears on that sorrel are twitching. Watch the flare of his nostrils."

It didn't take long before Daniel realized that Moody was right. "Hey, maybe it's someone's gonna help us," he whispered. "If they was a friend to the Mexicans, wouldn't they come right on in?" And then Daniel's eyes widened in excitement. "Maybe Jake's out there!"

"Jake doesn't even know we're in Mexico. I hate to tell you now, but I never did send that telegram we talked about, so stop wishing and start thinking. At a time like this you need to have a plan on what you're going to do when the bullets start flying."

"I know I'm going to shoot that one tall Mex over there. I don't like his looks a'tall. He stares at me too much and always has that sneer on his mutt-ugly face."

Moody smiled. "Well, that's a good plan, but you need to know in advance how you're going to get some cover and not be just sitting and staring about like a cow chewing its cud."

"You know, Moody, you really got me riled up here. For all you know it's only a javelina or a coyote slinking around out there that's got the horses nerved up," Daniel said.

"Maybe. But I've only lived this long because I expect the worst."

Both men sat without speaking for a spell. Finally Daniel said, "You know, Richard, one thing I been wondering about. I been wondering why we're here. I mean, there's plenty of law-breakers in Arizona we could be chasing after. What makes these two men so important that you're determined to track them down?"

"It's only Floyd Baker I want," Moody said after several minutes.

"Great. We're down here in hell 'cause Floyd Baker did you wrong and you need to even things up?"

"Something like that," Moody said, straining to see into the darkness beyond the glow of the campfire. "It goes back a long way, in another place." He paused a moment, "You got a plan to protect yourself?"

"Yeah. I suppose I'll lay flat behind this excuse of a log we're sittin' on. You got any suggestions?"

"Your gun loaded?" Moody asked, leaning forward to get up.

"Of course."

Suddenly the report of a rifle shattered the quiet of the campsite. Stunned, Daniel sat stupidly staring in the direction of the gunfire for a moment before he gathered his wits enough to roll behind the tiny chunk of mesquite he'd been perched on.

He looked quickly about and saw the Mexicans rousing themselves. Moody sprawled on the ground only a few feet away. Daniel drew his weapon and fired into the black night.

"Shoot a Mexican," Moody groaned. "You can at least *see* them!"

"Right. Right," and Daniel aimed at the nearest man – the tall one, firing three times, but hitting the man only once. "Shit! I only wounded him!" Daniel looked toward Moody for a reprimand and momentarily froze. Richard Moody lay on his back, a growing bloodstain spreading on his shirt. Immediately adrenaline pumped through the young marshal's body. He quickly got to his knees and began shooting at the Mexicans who were blindly firing their own weapons into the dark. The tall one finally toppled forward after a cartridge hit him in the back of the head. The older one, the one named Poncho, turned and saw his partner on the ground. As he did so, he became aware of the silence. Daniel also recognized that the gunman in the dark hadn't ever returned any fire. He'd fired only one round.

His hands shaking, Daniel tried to reload his weapon as the Mexican moved toward him. He saw Poncho's hate-filled face glare at him as the man fired his revolver wildly. Daniel feared death at any moment. Suddenly three quick shots rang out, and the marshal turned and saw Moody had rolled onto his stomach, his outstretched arm holding a gun. All three bullets entered Poncho's head as he toppled backward.

Then a voice rang out. "Richard Moody, I'm here for you. I've waited a long time for this and I intend on enjoying every minute watching you die." The stranger stood on the outside of the campsite, his rifle aimed at Moody. Glancing at Daniel, the man ordered, "Throw down that weapon, kid, and put those hands up or I'll kill you too."

"Leave the kid out of this, McGraw. This is between you and me. The kid has no part in it. He doesn't even know me." Richard looked over to Daniel and quietly said, "You edge on over and get on a horse and get the hell out of here, you hear me?"

Daniel began slowly backing away, hands up, as ordered.

"Come on, Moody. Stand up and face me like a man."

"Like your son faced Jake Silver? Like that? Like you gunned down Betsy Silver?" Moody taunted, holding his side as he slowly and unsteadily got to his feet.

"Throw down the gun, Moody. Don't embarrass yourself. You're in no position to outdraw me, and you know it's empty," McGraw said, a note of triumph in his voice. "And that woman's name was Betsy McGraw, you bastard. Silver never married her and he never would. She was nothing but a pretty, little whore."

Richard stood, noticeably weaving. "Tell you what, McGraw, I'll let you draw first, and I'll still kill you. I have one cartridge left."

McGraw laughed loudly. "You got a lot of nerve, I'll give you that."

By now Daniel had backed to a large, scrubby cactus where he thought he'd seen one of Moody's revolvers laying in the dirt. He figured the gun had flown from Moody's hand when the impact of the gunman's bullet knocked him to the ground…or in all the commotion earlier when he'd been shot, had Moody tossed it there for him to find?

He stood still and watched the two men for a moment, listening to their verbal banter. Moody swayed as if ready to pass out, and McGraw seemed to relish every minute of his enemy's last moments.

Infuriated by McGraw's sneaky tactics, Daniel could not contain his anger. He dove for the revolver, emitting a growl of fury. Through maddened senses he saw McGraw look his direction then quickly raise his rifle and momentarily hesitate, as though deciding whether to take aim at him or Moody. Daniel grabbed for the gun, dozens of sharp barbs biting into his hand. Oblivious to the pain, he rolled and fired, and rolled and fired again. And again. McGraw staggered backward a few steps then dropped heavily to the ground. Daniel stood and emptied the revolver into Ben McGraw's twitching body.

"Yeah. That was pretty good, Daniel. Pretty damn good," Moody said in a weak voice as he eased onto his hands and knees and slowly slumped onto the ground.

Daniel, still holding the revolver as though it were loaded, looked around at the display of dead bodies. Convinced they were all dead, he moved to Richard's side.

"Load up and check them over, kid. Never trust a man who looks dead. Gather their weapons," Moody half whispered, "any question about it, put another bullet in 'em."

"Richard, they're dead!" Daniel insisted. "Where're you hit?"

"It's my side. Damn good thing I stood up when I did or he'd have nailed me in the head."

"Shit! Your side. Okay. Let me see," Daniel said, not at all certain what to do.

"Kid, nothing you can do. Check those men. Get their weapons. Then get on a horse and get the hell out of here."

"I'm not leaving you, Richard Moody, so shut the hell up. I'm the boss now, so quit giving orders."

Weak as he was, Moody smiled at Daniel's response.

"Now, I'm going to check these men over, then I'm gathering their weapons. We'll fix that wound up and I'll take you to a doctor somewhere. Do they have doctors down here?"

"Horse doctors, maybe," Moody said, trying not to laugh.

"Fine time for a sense of humor," Daniel said as he picked up weapons and looked the dead men over. "Okay," he said after collecting the firearms. "You got the experience here. How do I fix this wound?"

"You need to wrap something around my middle. Get me on a horse if you can. I think I can sit well enough to travel," Moody said, closing his eyes and starting to murmur.

"In case you pass out, where do I go?"

"Head to San Felipe. It's closest. If nothing else, Diego Fuentes will be there and give me a proper burial," Moody said, groaning as a chuckle escaped. "Just keep on this road. When you see the gulf, go right. It's a well-worn road. It'll be hard to miss."

"How far to San Felipe?"

"Maybe two days if you ride straight through," Moody answered as Daniel began wrapping a torn shirt around his mid-section. "Maybe more. Maybe less. Can't remember all that well," Moody mumbled, slurring his words.

"No napping, Moody. We're making tracks, as you're so fond of saying," Daniel said, growing calm and confident. "I'm going to saddle two of the horses. Somehow none of the animals broke free, which is a miracle. Then I'll help you up."

After several attempts, Daniel finally hoisted Moody into the saddle. "I think I best tie you in. You're not looking too chipper," he said to the wounded man.

"Grab some grub, kid. Water. Take some guns. You may need them. Turn the other horses loose. They'll most likely follow us."

"What about the bodies?"

"Bodies? I don't see any," Moody said, his eyes closed and head bent low. "And Daniel, if I don't make it, just get the hell out of this country as soon as you can. You should be doing that now. And tell Jake that McGraw is dead. He's going to be mighty upset that it wasn't him who killed that monster, so tell him I did it or he's likely to beat the tar out of you."

Daniel mounted then said, "You're right, Moody, I don't feel the least bit bad about killing these men."

13

Concerned that the gunfire might have attracted a roving group of bandits, Cleary did not tarry. As though on a swivel, his head rotated continuously as he kept a sharp lookout ahead as well as behind. Every time he turned to look behind him, though, he saw Moody slumped over, swaying in the saddle. The young marshal perspired from the heat yet felt cold from fear of what might happen next. He tried talking to Moody, but the gunman's eyes only fluttered briefly in response.

Tense and worried, Cleary rode through the long night and watched the sky slowly turn light in the east. He had no idea how long they'd been traveling when he finally saw a glimpse of blue water ahead. Judging by the position of the sun, he reckoned it was late morning – certainly not yet noon. "Hey, Moody, I see the water. The gulf. I'll be looking for that road now," he said, mostly to reassure himself.

"You know," he continued, feeling a bit relieved at actually finding the gulf, "now that you're not talking much, I figure it's my one opportunity to tell you what's been on my mind. Maybe it's not right, my talking bad to you when you're feeling so poorly, but at least you won't be interrupting me," he said, turning to check on Moody. He wasn't sure if he truly saw the gunman's lips twitch like he might be trying to smile, or he merely wanted to see the gunman show some kind of awareness and imagined a small smile.

"Here's the way I figure this, sir. You got me all the way down here, and if you have the bad luck to die I'm in a real bad spot. Not speaking the language and all, nor knowing the customs, just isn't real helpful. Now, I'll give you this, you gave me plenty of opportunity to go back to Prescott by myself – with my tail between my legs, of course. No self-respectin' man would abandon his partner, and you know that, and you figured I'd stay with you, which I did. I'll admit it right up front. Fair and square I made the decision to stay. No argument there," Cleary admitted, trying to think things through and not get lost in his tangled web of thoughts. "So, that's only fair of me to own up to that. But, you were never very honest about why you were so hell-bent on following these fellers down here. All along I'm thinking it's 'cause they were just outlaws, but no. Now I learn you got a vendetta against one of 'em. Now that just doesn't seem right to drag a stranger, like me, into your personal vendetta." Cleary stopped talking, pleased with what he'd gotten off his chest.

The horses slowed as the heat of the day increased, but Cleary refused to stop and rest them. As Moody had predicted, the Mexicans' horses followed along, so the young man figured he could always change horses if necessary, although he wasn't sure Moody could take the jostling. The wound in Richard's side appeared to have stopped bleeding, though. The shirt wrapped about his waist no longer showed fresh seepage.

Within an hour or two, Cleary saw the road leading south that Moody had described. The breeze from the gulf now cooled the air and made travel easier. In fact, had Moody not lingered near death, Cleary thought he might have enjoyed this part of the journey. Except for his brief stay in San Diego, never before had Daniel seen a body of water so large that he couldn't land. And the gulf air had a freshness that he'd never before smelled. Sometimes the breeze felt cool and refreshing; the next moment a brisk wind blew warm. But always there was a strange tang in the air. Far out he could see small fishing boats bobbing on the swells. "Well, I never…." he muttered. "Too bad you can't enjoy this, Richard. It's quite a sight."

The well-worn road encouraged Cleary to continue traveling and not stop for the night. He briefly halted once to unsaddle his mount and saddle up one of the other horses, but he left Moody on the same mount, concerned that trying to get the gunman off his horse and on another would cause the bleeding to resume.

"As I was sayin' earlier, Richard, I haven't appreciated the way you've treated me on this trip. You've talked to me like I'm a kid. And another thing, Jake told me you had a great sense of humor and I have yet to hear you say one funny thing worth laughing at," Cleary paused for a few minutes. "And I do have one more thing to say while I'm at it, Richard Moody. If you die on me, I have no idea how to get your dead carcass back to Arizona, so you better not die. And that's an order, goddamn it. I've been scared half witless since we got into this country, thanks to you, and I'm not going to put up with this much longer."

As the hours passed Cleary's confidence grew. Hadn't he come this far and survived? Hadn't he killed a man? Maybe two? Shot them plain dead. Granted, the first time he only wounded one, but after that, even the threat of hell couldn't stop him, and he puffed a bit with pride at the memory. Now he could say he'd ridden with Mexican outlaws, fought them, and survived, thanks to Richard's counsel. Maybe Moody had done okay at preparing him for the ordeals awaiting. After all, he'd become a much better tracker under Moody's tutelage while pursuing Baker and McKinney down the Colorado. Moody claimed he wasn't much of a tracker. Said Jake Silver had taught him pretty much most of what he knew, which was far more than Daniel had known.

Once in San Felipe, however – if not before – he'd have the big Mexican to contend with… somehow. He had Floyd Baker and Jarvis McKinney to arrest and drag back to Arizona. He had Moody to deal with – however that might turn out. Cleary wasn't so confident that he couldn't admit he could use some help, but he no longer felt so fearful. Looking at the entire situation, he realized he should avoid getting entangled with Fuentes unless forced to. His concern would be with

Baker and McKinney, and primarily with Baker since that man was the worst of the two and also an enemy of Richard's. "So, really, I only have two problems," Cleary spoke softly to Moody. "I have Baker, and I have you – well, I gotta get out of Mexico too, but I'll manage that somehow, if Baker doesn't get to me first. Or your good Mexican buddy."

As the horses plodded on into the night, Cleary dozed in the saddle, for when the sun rose he awoke and saw the small town of San Felipe in the distance and what looked to be another horseman far ahead. "Moody, we got maybe twenty miles to go," Cleary announced blinking rapidly to clear his eyes. "I think I just seen San Felipe when we were coming down that slope."

Moody, now entirely slumped over the saddle, his head on the horse's neck, remained silent.

"Damn, I never thought I'd miss hearing your nagging voice and lectures, but I surely do."

Floyd Baker gained consciousness several days after most everyone who tended to him figured he'd be dead in a day, two at most. The blurry world confused Baker, and his head ached something awful. "Am I dead yet?" he asked the man who'd last looked in on him.

The stranger rattled something off in gibberish and then quickly left the room. Baker could hear the man jabbering in the hallway, but couldn't figure out what in the world he was saying. Exhausted, he slipped into a light sleep, wincing with every pounding beat in his head. At some point he felt the presence of someone in the room. Slowly he forced his eyes open, but he could not make out any discernible features on the stranger.

Once his eyes opened, the man began to speak. "So, you have survived after all," an accented voice said. "Perhaps you can be of use to me. If not, I will kill you. So think about this."

Baker had no idea how long he'd slept, or how many days had passed. Finally he awoke, and his own stink nearly gagged him. He lay quite still, trying not to breathe deeply lest the foul odor in the room sickened him further. Judging by the soiled bed, he suspected he'd lain there for some days. Clearly no one had bothered to tend to him. "Hey!" he yelled. "Anybody hear me?" He paused and tried to clear his throat. "HEY!" he yelled louder. "I need some help in here! Someone!"

Remembering his pounding head, Baker hesitated to sit up lest his head fall off, or blow up, which is what it had felt like it would do the last time he awoke. After several minutes elapsed and no one answered his call, Baker cautiously worked himself into a sitting position. Instantly dizzy, he closed his eyes and held onto the side of the bed for a few minutes. "I need help in here!" he bellowed.

Where the hell is McKinney? Why hasn't he taken care of me? Baker wondered. "Jarvis! Jarvis! Help me!"

Slowly Baker laid back down, his head again aching from the effort of yelling. *Damn! I'm gonna die in this hellhole if someone don't get in here and give me a hand,* he thought as he closed his eyes and waited for the pains to subside. "Jeesh I stink. I smell like I'm already half dead," he muttered.

"Yes, amigo, you stink like an old, dead, rotting carcass," a big Mexican said, standing in the doorway.

Baker slowly turned his head to look at the intruder. "Who the hell are you? You own this here establishment? What kinda place you run? How's a man get any help around here?"

"I will send someone to help you. Then I will cut your tongue out for speaking so disrespectfully to me," the Mexican replied. "Like most Americanos, you have no manners. Perhaps I will teach you some, or perhaps I will feed you to the wild dogs like I did your friend."

A few minutes later, four armed men stormed into Baker's room. Blathering rapidly to each other, each man grabbed an arm or a leg, and they roughly carried him down the stairs and across the street where they tossed him into a stone water trough.

Baker's body screamed in agony but no sound came from his paralyzed throat. His broken bones had not been set, and several had not yet mended. For the first time since he could remember, tears coursed down his whiskered, filthy face. "Please," he begged. "Help me. Oh Lord, help me!"

The four men laughed at Baker's gyrations as he wallowed about and tried to sit upright, gasping for air. They shouted at him and mimicked him until the big man stood among them. "Get him out," the man ordered. "Get those stinking clothes off him, then take him to the cantina."

Baker passed out from the pain of being pulled from the pool of water. He awoke a short time later, and after several moments of confusion as he stared at the ceiling, he saw he was lying naked on a table in a cantina. Half-a-dozen or so armed Mexicans filled the room. No one spoke or moved to help him.

Then the big man approached and looked at him with disgust written on his face. "You still stink. You have laid in your own filth for days. Bugs cover your body. You are not fit to feed to my dogs."

"Well, beggin' your pardon, but I don't know what happened here. I musta got hurt, I reckon. Don't know where my partner is, but if you'll let me up, I'll get on my clothes and be on my way. Won't never come back neither," Baker whimpered, his heart pounding.

The big man sighed heavily. "What to do with you – what to do. That is my problem. Your friend? You see, he was easy. Even his bones are probably devoured by now. Why should I not kill you also?" he asked. "Come. Give me a good answer and perhaps I will let you live." The Mexican winked at those around him and they dutifully laughed.

Floyd Baker had never been the underdog. He laid there, eyes wide and mouth open, searching his empty brain for an answer that might spare his life. He looked about and saw the Mexicans, all well-dressed and heavily armed, and he realized these were men he could not buffalo with his foul talk and threats. "Tell you what, mister," he finally said, "you let me live, and I will work for you. I'll do whatever you tell me. I'm a gunman. I'm pretty fast. Maybe not now, but when I'm well, I'm one of the fastest guns you'll ever see."

The Mexican shrugged. "The desert is filled with fast gunmen," he said, "and all of them are dead." The big man pulled up a chair and sat. "Why are you here? You Americanos are not welcome in my country. You come and you rape our women, even our little girls, and you steal, you kill my countrymen. Do not deny. The people of San Felipe have told me so."

"That was all a big mistake. That was my partner's idea. Not mine."

The Mexican pulled a long knife from his waistband. "You lie. Now you leave me no choice but to cut your tongue out," and he nodded to several men who stood nearby.

"No! I swear to you! I will tell the truth! I came here to escape the lawdogs that were hounding me. I got into trouble in Arizona. I admit I did a few bad deeds," Baker cried, shaking so hard his bones knocked against the wooden table as the men approached to hold him down. "My partner and I were hiding out down here until it was safe to go back. I swear. I swear on my mother's grave!" Baker said, his voice breaking. "I'll go on back today. Right now, I promise," he pleaded as tears ran down his cheeks.

Suddenly Baker became aware of a change in the room. As he'd been speaking, the men surrounding him had all started looking toward the door. One man would nudge another, and then that man would do likewise, until all who'd been gathered around him were looking at someone or something that had just entered the room. Baker couldn't make out what was happening because of the men standing in his way, but he saw the big Mexican slowly stand, and a large smile spread across his face.

For a moment no one moved, and then the big man said, “Jake Silver.” And he moved toward the newcomer in the room. “Jake Silver. I am glad to see you have come.”

The room started to break into pandemonium, but the head Mexican raised his hand and demanded silence. “Get this man out of here,” he ordered, nodding toward Baker. “Don’t kill him yet. The rest of you leave.” Then the Mexican clasped the man’s hand, and again he said, “Jake Silver.”

14

Jake Silver and Diego Fuentes stood, each with his eyes locked on the other, their hands in a tight grip. After several moments, Diego released Jake's hand.

"Come," Diego finally said. "Let us sit," and he moved to a different table and pulled out two chairs, pushing one toward Jake. "Pablo, bring us food. Pronto," he called to a man who'd retreated only to a far corner, not from the room as the rest had.

Pablo nodded but hesitated.

"Everything is fine, Pablo," Diego assured him, not taking his eyes off Jake. "Go."

Jake remained silent, so Diego spoke. "It is good to see you, amigo. Very good."

"Amigo? The last time I saw you, Diego, you swore you'd kill me the next time we met."

"Yes, well, I was much disturbed by your friend. And, of course, you too. You betrayed me. But, let's not talk of old wounds. For now, let me take a good look at my friend," Diego said.

"I haven't changed much, Diego."

"Yes, my friend, I think you have," Diego said after a few moments. "You are not the same man who lived in my house all those months. The truth is in your eyes. You never were very good at hiding what you were thinking – or feeling," Diego said, smiling. "Even now you are thinking if you should draw your weapon, or if you should surrender and let me kill you. Perhaps you have lost your reason to live. The old Jake would not have thought of such things." Diego stopped speaking as Pablo set a bottle of Tequila and two glasses on the table then turned away. "I hear about your woman," Diego continued after Pablo left the room. "The man who shot her lives nearby, did you know this?" Diego asked.

Jake nodded.

"But of course you did. So, I must ask, are you here to kill the McGraw man who shot your beautiful woman? Or are you here to rescue your friend who is even now en route to San Felipe?"

"Perhaps both," Jake replied. "I knew McGraw was here, but I came to get Richard Moody, just as he came to get me when you kept me captive all those months."

"Captive? No my friend. You were my guest. I saved your life. I treated you well. You lived in luxury in my hacienda. I gave you women. Food. The things every man wants and needs and aches for. Your debt to me was great, and it remains so."

"Yes, Diego. And I saved your life when we met in the desert."

Diego shrugged. "That was only a little save. I gave you your life back, my friend. You were pouring blood when I found you."

"You think I still owe you?"

"I'm thinking you do, amigo. And you will have your chance to pay me once and for all when Moody arrives and you kill him. That was our bargain back then. It is my offer once again," Diego said, leaning back in his chair with a big smile on his face. "But first, I will let you kill McGraw. Then you kill Moody. You see? You will satisfy your need for revenge against McGraw, and then you will satisfy my need for revenge – and, of course, repayment for your life." Diego looked from Jake to Pablo, who entered at that moment with a platter of tamales.

"So, we eat and talk. Let us not ruin good food by arguing. It will be as I say."

Jake smiled. He'd almost forgotten how direct and simple things were for Diego. There was never any middle ground with the man. No negotiation. The law was simply based on his word, whim, and logic. And it was always final.

"So, you tell me how you came to be in San Felipe," Diego said after washing down two tamales with a shot of tequila. "You come through the wet land?"

"I came from Puerto Penasco," Jake replied. "Paid a fisherman to take me and my horse across the gulf. Sure as hell won't do that again."

Diego laughed. "In your heart you must desire the sea," he said. "Two times now you come to my country on a boat."

"It was a helluva rough trip from Penasco," Jake said, helping himself to another tamale. "I don't think I'll be going to sea again for a long, long time – if ever."

"So, tell me," Diego began, pushing his plate away. "Why is your friend coming all this way for two Americanos not worth the carcass of a dead dog?"

Jake shrugged. "Diego, I'm a bit confused about that myself. Makes no sense at all. Baker and McKinney are just two outlaws among hundreds roaming the west," Jake said, taking another tamale. "They're worse than most, I'll grant that. They've done their share of stealing and killing, even kidnapped a young girl. Baker's far worse than McKinney, but still, neither is worth the trek all the way down here."

"I had McKinney fed to the wild dogs already," Diego said, matter-of-factly. "The man called Baker has been mostly dead but has come back to life, as they say. Not so lively right now, but perhaps the evil in him keeps him from dying."

"Was that Baker on the table when I came in?" Jake asked.

Diego nodded. "*Si*. I was about to cut out his tongue."

Jake sighed. "Good food, Diego. I haven't eaten much since I left Penasco," he said as he pushed away from the table. "So, let's lay our cards on the table. Nothing has changed. I'm not going to shoot my friend. Just like I didn't shoot you when I left you in the desert, I won't shoot Richard."

"Yes, Jake, I think you will. I am a gambling man, and I am betting that you will fire at Richard Moody."

"You know he's faster than me, Diego. Much faster. He'll shoot me. You won't get your revenge."

"But I will, Jake Silver. If the man shoots you, my good friend, I will have his fingers ripped from his hands and his skin slowly peeled from his body. You will disappoint me, amigo, if you do not kill him before he kills you. Then, when you have killed him, your debt is cancelled and your betrayal forgiven," Diego said. "You come to my hacienda as my guest, not my captive as you like to say!" Fuentes beamed with pleasure.

Suddenly the batwing doors flew open and Mateo rushed into the room. "Senor Diego, two Americanos come," Mateo shouted, so excited he could barely speak. "One looks to be dead. The other wears a badge and is riding a horse with your mark, the mark of Fuentes. I think he is the Americano you are waiting for, but Poncho and Juan are not seen! They do not ride with the Americanos," Mateo exclaimed, breathing heavily.

Jake watched Diego's face turn fiercely angry as the big Mexican upended the table and strode from the room. Jake followed immediately, his hand inadvertently checking for his gun. Diego had not taken it – a grave oversight.

Thirsty and exhausted, Daniel Cleary rode into San Felipe, the lead line of the horse carrying Richard Moody looped around his saddle horn. He proceeded up what looked to be the sandy main street in the small, three street town, asking Mexicans hovering for safety in doorways where he could find a doctor. The onlookers stared mutely at the crazed rider.

Suddenly a large group of armed men swarmed into the street, barring his progress.

"Doctor! Doctor? I need a doctor here. Does anyone here speak American?" Cleary asked through parched lips.

No one spoke, but several drew their weapons. Exasperated, Daniel cursed loudly. He sat there swearing and wondering what to do, when the crowd of men parted and another Mexican, the leader by all appearances, strode through the gathering.

"Are you the doctor?" Cleary asked hesitantly, already knowing the answer.

"I am Diego Fuentes."

This is it, Cleary thought. *It's all over now.*

"Where are my men? The ones who were to ride with you?" Diego asked as he drew his weapon and aimed at Cleary.

Cleary sat, dumbfounded. Too tired to react, he simply said, "I need a doctor for this man."

At that moment Jake Silver shoved his way through the crowd of men. "Daniel, what in hell happened?" he asked as he rushed to Moody's horse.

"McGraw bushwhacked us, Marshal. He shot Moody, and then…" Daniel paused. Even though nearly in a stupor, he realized if he admitted that he and Moody shot the two Mexican guards it would be the end of them. "And then McGraw shot the two Mexican men traveling with us." He saw Jake's skeptical look but continued. "That McGraw came out of nowhere in the dead of night, Marshal. I'm lucky to be alive."

"Where's this McGraw now?" Fuentes interrupted.

"He's dead. I shot him. Many times."

"You're telling me you killed McGraw?" Jake asked, his jaw tense and eyes narrowed.

"Well, I'm supposed to tell you that Moody shot him."

Jake stood motionless for a moment before he spoke. "Help me get Richard off this horse, Daniel. He's still alive." Turning to Diego, Jake said, "He needs a doctor. Is there a doctor around here?"

Diego nodded. "Not a doctor as you know them, but there is a man who tends to wounds and animals. He'll have to do." Then he turned to several of his men and issued an order. "Take him into the cantina for now, and you, Julio, find the old medicine man. Bring him at once. As for you," he said, looking at Daniel Cleary, "I will take your weapon now or I kill you where you stand."

Daniel looked to Jake, who nodded for him to do as directed.

"I will take your weapon, too, my friend," Diego said, turning to Jake. "You will not escape me this time. If Moody dies, then you will earn your freedom by killing this boy who rode in with him. I think he has not been truthful about my men." Diego smiled at Jake. "Don't think to draw on me, amigo."

Jake looked around and saw every man in attendance with his weapon pointed at him and Daniel.

"Now, you are my guests," Diego said as he handed the surrendered weapons to one of his people. "Feel free to wander about San Felipe as you wish. And Jake, you will not get lost this time," Diego said, a smirk on his happy face. "One or two of my men will accompany you at all times. Should you disappear, they will be buried alive. I know a good man like yourself would not want that on his conscience."

Diego turn to leave, but stopped. "Join me at sunset in the cantina like in the old days. We still have much to discuss."

Jake and Daniel watched the big man walk away, flanked by his men. They stood in the deserted street a few seconds before either spoke. "Now what?" Daniel finally asked.

"Let's get you some food and some sleep, and then we'll talk," Jake said walking toward the ramshackle hotel.

"I can't sleep, Jake. How the hell can you talk about eating and sleeping at a time like this! You gonna draw on me if it comes down to it?" Cleary asked, shaken.

"I don't know, kid."

"What kind of answer is that? '*I don't know.*' That's not very damn reassuring."

Jake stopped and turned to Daniel who was several steps behind. "Listen, Daniel, the last thing you need is to get over-excited here. Get some sleep. Eat. Clean up. We'll make a plan later."

"Damn! I hate you and your stupid friend. Both of you are crazier than hell. What're you doing here, anyway?" Daniel asked.

"Came down here to save your ass."

The two entered the downtrodden adobe building and Jake grabbed a key off the wall, ignoring the attendant nervously wringing his hands. "Here. Go sleep. Don't do anything stupid," and he handed the key to Daniel. "The keys don't work, by the way. They're strictly for show."

At that moment, two of Diego's men entered the tiny lobby. Jake rattled something off in Spanish, and one of the men nodded. "Daniel," Jake said, "these are the bodyguards. Be nice to them for as long as possible. Nod and smile. We may have to kill them later."

"You got a plan already?" Daniel asked as he slowly started up the stairs to the second floor.

"Not yet. But something will happen. It always does," Jake answered. "Now, I'm going to check on Moody. I'll be back. Stay put."

Moody looked to be in bad shape. He'd been moved to a filthy bed in the back room of the cantina. As the Mexican horse doctor peeled back the blood-soaked shirt bound around the gunman's middle, the wound began to seep. Jake winced at the bruised, bloody hole in Moody's side.

Carefully the Mexican felt beneath Moody's side. He smiled and nodded. "The bullet passed through your friend," he said in Spanish. "Clean wound. Wait. Maybe he live."

"He damn well better live," Diego said, entering the room. "Your lucky day, Jake. Or maybe I should say the boy's lucky day. You should be able to outdraw your friend now, no?"

"Diego, that would be an insult to me if I killed him now," Jake said. "Even a woman could kill him now."

Diego nodded sagely. "True. I would not make you less a man. We wait. I am in no rush. We wait one week, two weeks. A month. Then you shoot him. Meanwhile, we eat, drink, talk of old times. I find you a new woman, huh, my friend? A beautiful Mexican girl? I find one for you. Make a new man of you." Diego smiled warmly. "Tonight! Tonight we have good food, tequila, and women. You and me. It will be like before all this trouble began. Ah! We will cut Baker's tongue out tonight too. Feed it to the dogs!" Diego left the room, whistling happily.

Jake stayed for several hours, watching Moody breathe. The horse doctor left and soon returned with prickly pear ointment. Next he made a poultice of cactus gel and applied it to Richard's wound. Then he worriedly paced about, spooning very small amounts of some kind of stinky liquid into the gunman's mouth from time to time.

Jake could think of no logical explanation why Moody had come so far for such a lowdown, dirty-dog as Floyd Baker. Unless Moody had come for Fuentes. That was the only other possible explanation. But why drag Daniel Cleary into the mess? Jake somehow didn't think the answer was Fuentes, at least not the entire answer. Something else had motivated Moody to go to such an extreme.

Jake dozed fitfully in his chair, worry about his young marshal heavy on his mind in his waking moments. How could he get Cleary out of San Felipe? There was no way the young man could escape by land. Fuentes had too many men, and they all knew the territory. No, it would have to be by sea if escape was possible at all. Jake would refuse to draw on Cleary. Thc boy was good with a gun, but nowhere in the same league as he and Moody. No, he'd have to do some exploring along the bay. Find a boat. Maybe pay a fisherman to take the boy across the gulf in the dead of night. Risky. Word would already be around San Felipe not to help the Americans. Then there were the two Mexicans following two steps behind him.

He awoke to someone shaking his shoulder and looked up to see Cleary standing by his chair.

"You get any sleep?"

"Yeah. A little," Daniel answered. "I'm better than I was, anyway." Daniel pulled up a chair. "How's he doing?"

"Hard to tell. He's just been sleeping." Jake turned to face Daniel. "What the hell went on out there, Daniel?"

Cleary shook his head in dismay. "It was a mess from the start, Jake," he said, slumping in his chair. "Baker and McKinney left a string of bodies all the way to Yuma. We were usually a day, maybe two behind them. We finally got to Yuma, then Moody said he had to go to San Diego. He never told me what he was going to do there, but I went with him anyway. From there we left for Tijuana. Moody got word that the two men were in San Felipe, so then we left for San Felipe and got joined by these two Mexican bandits who Moody said were sent by Fuentes to 'protect us.' Then out of nowhere one night McGraw showed up and shot Moody. Moody managed to kill the big Mexican and I shot the other one and McGraw. A dozen times." Daniel paused. "It's been a helluva trip."

"Daniel, did you ever figure out why Moody was so willing to go to such lengths to get Baker and McKinney?"

"I asked him about that the night before McGraw attacked. It has something to do with Baker. Something from the past. He didn't go into detail, but I got the feeling that it was some kind of vendetta."

"I wondered about that," Jake said. "Listen, kid, I'm not going to lie to you. We're in a bit of a mess here. I'm going to try to get you out, if at all possible. I have an idea that might work. I'll stay here with Moody."

"I'm not leaving you guys," Daniel said, straightening up in his chair. "I'm not a coward, Jake. I won't leave until you two leave," he said, determination in his voice.

"Daniel, you have no idea how ruthless Diego Fuentes can be. Ruthless. He's going to cut Baker's tongue out tonight, okay? That's the kind of stuff he does. He already fed McKinney to the wild dogs in the desert. When he says he's going to have a man skinned alive, it happens," Jake said with emphasis. "You don't need to be here for this. Moody and I have a past with Fuentes. You don't."

"Well, I guess it's like Moody told me, 'A coward dies many times; a brave man dies but once.'"

"Don't listen to the crap that comes out of that man's mouth," Jake scoffed. "He likes the sound of his own voice."

"He sure didn't talk much with me. Glared at me. Ignored me. Lectured me. But not much friendly chat."

"Consider yourself lucky. He can quote from any man who ever lived."

"'It is nothing to die. It is frightful not to live,'" Moody muttered in a broken voice. "Victor Hugo said that, you illiterates."

Jake looked at the wan figure on the bed. "He speaks," Jake said. Smiling, he put his hand on Moody's shoulder and squeezed it. "Good to see you alive, Mr. Moody. Good to see you alive."

15

One week passed. Then two. Floyd Baker's recovery progressed rapidly except for the violent headaches that came on without provocation. Baker tried treating the migraines with whiskey, but when that didn't work he used opium. Often he retreated to an opiate dealer on the edge of town for several days to escape the ceaseless pounding in his head. When not drugged or in excruciating pain, he kept a close watch to avoid Diego Fuentes, and he kept his foul mouth closed lest Fuentes remembered that he hadn't removed his tongue.

Baker also spent time practicing his draw. Because his shoulder, wrist, and several fingers had been injured – if not broken – in the donkey incident, his draw was now slow and awkward. He wouldn't last a minute if he left Mexico and had to defend himself against the law, or any other outlaw for that matter. Baker's bodyguard, a mean-looking, swarthy man named Jorge, allowed him to practice with an unloaded weapon. Some of the men would gather in the evenings to watch Baker work on his 'pistolero'. At first his efforts looked downright pathetic and the Mexicans jeered at him and laughed loudly, but slowly he gained some speed – nothing like his glory days, however.

Baker feared he would have to face Richard Moody before the drama taking place in San Felipe ended, and Moody was fast. Moody had reason to want to kill him, too.

Richard Moody also was recovering. His gunshot wound had healed well, although he'd had his doubts when the horse doctor applied a foul-smelling ointment to the wound. Despite the tenderness in his side and back, Moody eagerly left the filthy bed in the back of the cantina and took a room next to Jake's at the now nearly-packed hotel. It seemed the sleepy little town of San Felipe had become a popular spot when news of the impending duels became known.

Moody also began practicing his draw. He would kill Floyd Baker, but he would not kill Jake Silver. He'd made up his mind. Jake had a daughter who needed him, and a nephew. A job. Moody had no one and nothing.

"Richard, remember when we were up on the rim, and I asked you how you got into the gunslinger life? You never answered. Said you'd talk about it later," Jake said, watching Moody's face for a sign of remembrance. "Is Floyd Baker part of the past that brought you to this point? I'd like to know," Jake continued. "You've dragged Cleary into a mess here. If this is a personal vendetta, that wasn't the best decision you've ever made."

"I agree. It was a bad decision. I tried, Jake, to get that damn kid to leave. Tried several times. I suppose I should have taken off in the middle of the night." Moody said. "But what makes you think I have revenge on my mind?"

"There's no other logical explanation for why you returned to this godforsaken country. Surely you aren't after Fuentes."

Moody didn't answer for many minutes, so Jake was surprised when he began talking. "Yes. I came here for Baker. I've been looking for him for a long time. Not looking hard like at first, but I've had my eye out for him," Moody said, signaling for another round of drinks. "I knew that eventually our paths would cross unless someone did him in before I got to him."

Jake got up and retrieved the two beers that the Mexican barkeep was too lazy to deliver to their table. Moody took a long drink before he continued. "Nice of Fuentes to pay for all the food and drinks," he commented sarcastically. "Anyway, as for Baker, yeah, I'll kill him. I should've done it a long time ago."

"So what's your beef with him?" Jake asked.

"I left home early. I think I told you. Took off. I couldn't face my mother again after what Baker did to her." Moody held the glass so tightly in his hand that Jake thought it might break.

"Baker and I went to school together. He was a year or two older than I was. He quit about the fourth or fifth grade, I guess. Wasn't much of a student anyway. Even then, as young as I was, that was evident. Mainly he just made trouble. He picked on kids – little kids. He and I got into it a few times about that, and usually he beat me up pretty good. Even then he was a lot bigger than I was. He was a mean one, Jake. Just down and out mean and ornery. There was no accounting for it." Moody shook his head in anger. "Anyway, he came over to our ranch one day to beat me up again, but I'd gone off. I was around twelve or thirteen, I think. My mom was home alone. She was a small gal, very attractive. When he found out no one was around, he barged in. He raped her that day and beat her up pretty bad. Katherine was just a little girl and she saw it all. I'm not sure if she remembered it. Like I said, she was awful young. Thankfully he didn't do anything to her. Then for some reason, he just ran off. Left town. Disappeared."

"I'm sorry to hear that," Jake said, beginning to understand why Moody had taken the pursuit of Baker so seriously.

"Anyway, I couldn't stay home. I got my uncle to move in with ma and I left. She was never the same, Jake. My leaving probably didn't help her, I know that now. But at the time I felt responsible for what happened to her. If I'd been home where I should've been…well, you know how kids think," Moody said, emptying his glass of beer. "In the back of my mind I've known the day would come when I'd kill him. In all honesty, I've thought about this moment for years. I've pictured where I'll put the cartridge in his body. In my mind I've seen him in the dirt, groveling."

"You'll have your chance, Richard, once Diego thinks you're both mended enough to make it a real contest. He's making a big fiesta out of all this."

"Well, I've heard Baker isn't doing too well. You know, don't you, that he was the fastest draw anybody had ever seen – at least according to everyone who ever saw him and lived to tell about it," Moody said, leaning back in his chair. "I'm disappointed I won't be going up against the 'fastest gun in the west'," he said, smiling. "It's kind of anti-climactic after all these years of waiting."

Jake only shook his head in response. "Be thankful. I've heard stories about Baker over the years. You're not looking up to par yourself, I hate to tell you."

Richard leaned in and said in a low voice, "I been faking it," and he burst into laughter.

Jake tried to safeguard Daniel Cleary from Diego's troublesome "soldiers" who seemed to enjoy heckling the young man. Surprised that Cleary showed no outward signs of fear, Jake was impressed. The boy seemed to have grown up somewhere between Prescott and San Felipe.

"I figure this way, Jake," Cleary said one afternoon when the two of them sat in the shade talking about the situation at hand, "there's no point in acting scared. It's not going to help. I'll admit I'm more than a bit anxious about the mess we're in, but I know I've got to keep my wits about me and not let those animals know how I really feel. My gut tells me if they sense weakness, they'll come in for the kill."

"You pretty much got it, Daniel."

"You got a plan yet to get us out of here alive?"

Jake shook his head. "Hate to tell you, but no, but I'm thinking about it all the time. The only possible escape I can see is by boat. Diego's men will hunt us down like animals if we try to leave by land. But every fisherman for miles knows better than to pick us up. Something'll come up though. I got a feeling about it."

Daniel laughed. "Richard told me about some of your escapades. It seemed like something always came along and saved your sorry asses."

Jake smiled as he chewed on the end of a match. "Yeah. That's true. We were lucky. Wish I could say it was my great planning and skill, but…."

Diego often summoned Jake to spend the afternoons and evenings in his company. The Mexican habitually waxed on endlessly about any subject that popped into his head. Jake mostly smiled and agreed with the big man's ravings. At least once in every session, however, Diego grew serious and reminisced about the many months Jake had lived under his roof in Guerrero Negro. "Those were the best times of my life amigo. I trusted you. You were the first and only man I have ever trusted. So refreshing that you weren't after my power, my land. But, then you betrayed me." And Diego would scowl as disappointment flooded his eyes.

After several weeks, Jake began to sense that things might soon come to a head. He could feel the tension in the town growing as the two notorious gunmen, Baker and Moody, began to move about more, sometimes meeting each other on the street. Neither man spoke to the other, but each glared with hatred at his opponent. Emotions grew tight as a violin string. Men placed bets, and then more bets. Sometimes the crowd favored Baker; other times Moody. No one, however, wagered on who would win in a Jake Silver showdown. The people in the small town took to Jake. He spoke their language fluently. He gave treats to their children. He even spent an afternoon helping a local resident re-thatch his palm-leaf roof. Diego Fuentes could see the fondness that his people had for his friend, and he began to question whether having him involved in gunplay was the best thing to do. He did not want to lose the favor of the people. What if Jake were to lose to Baker or to Moody? No, that could not be allowed.

Finally things unraveled on a hot night in the cantina. Lately both Moody and Baker had been present in the evenings. Neither acknowledged the other, but their joint presence had begun to affect the patrons who'd been waiting impatiently for the showdown. Jake sat at Fuentes' table near the door, as was demanded, while Cleary and Moody sat at a table in the center of the small room. Baker stood at the bar muttering to himself. Every person in San Felipe steered clear of the man who most thought to be crazed. Only his guard, Jorge, kept him company. More than one man wished Baker dead because of the vile acts he'd committed on their daughters.

Baker began to feel one of his headaches coming on, so he felt more short-tempered than usual. The tension of the last few weeks had grown almost unbearable. The fear of losing his tongue at the hands of Fuentes, the searing headaches, and seeing Moody moving about town with Jake Silver was taking its toll. He wanted his suffering to end. Killing Moody would cure him, he felt certain. Moody was likely responsible for the headaches, Baker reasoned, and Fuentes was bound to let him leave San Felipe once the showdown was over. Killing Moody would not be all that difficult. Baker knew his own draw was slower than it had been, but he felt confident that Moody would fold under pressure, just like he'd folded decades ago when he'd not been home on the day he knew he would be beat up – again.

Slowly Baker turned his back to the bar and leaned against it and stared at Moody. People noticed, and the crowd grew quiet. It wasn't long before Moody looked up, and Baker nodded. "It's time, you little runt. Or are you gonna try and run off again?"

Fuentes watched the encounter and smiled. "Yes," he whispered to Jake. Fuentes stood and walked to the center of the room. "Eduardo, give your weapon to Baker. Put only one bullet in the chamber. No, I change my mind. Make that two. Two bullets." Turning to another of his soldiers he said, "Fernando, give your weapon to Moody. Two bullets in the chamber."

Both men did as ordered and stepped back. Suddenly the entire crowd pressed itself against the adobe walls of the cantina. "No," Fuentes said. "We go to the plaza. More people can enjoy the spectacle." Turning to Moody and Baker, he said, "If you fire your weapon before I give the order, you will be skinned alive. And you," he said turning to Baker, "will first have your tongue cut out. Do not think I have forgotten."

Fuentes led the way to the town's small plaza with Baker and Moody directly behind him. Jake followed closely behind Moody, whispering encouragement. "Just remember, this guy is slow," Jake said. "He's not what he used to be. I've heard the Mexicans talking, Richard."

"Jake, you act like I've never done this before," Moody said, a small smile on his face. "Relax."

As though putting on a theatrical production, Diego Fuentes placed each gunman exactly where he thought they'd best be seen by the growing crowd. Then, he spoke to the assembly.

"My friends, you have here two most bad men," he said, turning first to Baker and pointing, then turning to Moody. "These are the kinds of men who come to my country, our country, and commit crimes. They steal. They kill. They ruin our women. They are pigs. To bring you justice, I will let them kill each other." The crowd cheered and shouted epithets at the two men. "Should one live," and here Diego paused for effect, "should one of these evil men live, that man will face Jake Silver." Diego waited for approval from the crowd, but only his own men showed interest.

"Now, I will step from this plaza and raise my arm. When I lower my arm, the men may draw and fire. Each man has two bullets. If they both miss, in an effort to avoid their punishment, they will be skinned alive and hanged. There is no escaping the wrath of Fuentes or the will of the people," he roared.

Diego stepped aside and slowly, dramatically, raised his right arm. He held it aloft for a full ten seconds in order to put everyone on edge, then he quickly dropped it.

Both men drew, and three shots rang out, but a practiced eye could see that Moody had the faster draw.

Baker slowly crumpled to the ground. Moody had fired a gut shot, knowing it to be excruciatingly painful. One of Baker's bullets grazed Moody's right shoulder; the other missed entirely. Moody's hope was that no one would be particularly attentive as to who fired two shots, especially since Baker's first shot had been wild. Slowly Moody approached Baker as he groaned and cursed. He stood over the prone man and kept the gun close to his side. He carefully opened the chamber with his index finger, allowing the chamber to open enough for the unused cartridge to fall loose at his feet. He looked to Jake who nodded slightly. Jake then knelt by Baker's body, his knee covering Moody's second cartridge.

"Yep. Afraid you're done for, Mr. Baker," Jake said, putting his hand on the ground by his knee and bending over Baker's body, as though interested in the wound. "Looks pretty bad to me. I'll give you a few days at most," he said as he slowly pushed himself up. "Happy to say you're gonna have a lot of pain." He held the cartridge between two fingers as he stood, then he casually slid his fingers into his trouser pocket for a moment. "You want a priest or something?"

"You bastard!" Baker uttered through clenched teeth. "You'll get yours when your good friend shoots you. Damn you both to hell, anyway!"

"Well, I guess I'll see you there, then," Jake replied, slowly moving aside so Baker could be carried elsewhere.

"Don't bother taking him inside," Fuentes said, stepping through the crowd. "Take him to the desert and leave him. Fresh blood is always welcome to the animals."

As money exchanged hands a few fisticuffs broke out. After the skirmishes the crowd dispersed. Some went home, but most returned to the cantina to rehash the evening's event.

Only Moody and Silver remained standing in the plaza, their guards nearby.

"You get a bit scraped there?" Jake asked, looking at the tear in Moody's suit coat. "You okay?"

"Just a scratch. It's nothing."

"Good move with the extra cartridge. Now we'll have all of five bullets in our showdown, assuming we both get two. We'll need more than that if we're going to do much damage around here."

Moody nodded. "I'm just hoping Fuentes doesn't get the idea to put one of us up against Cleary. The kid's accurate, but he's not as fast as either of us. I don't want to kill that kid, Jake."

"You're right. We may need to do something drastic if that's Fuentes' plan," Jake said.

"Diego will save you for last. You better start thinking." Moody turned to leave, "See you in the morning, Jake."

16

Moody returned to his room and removed his coat. "Damn that Baker," he muttered looking at the rip in the suit. The shirt was likewise slightly torn, and his shoulder bore a long scratch.

I was slow on the draw, Moody thought. *No excuses. Just plain slow. Damn good thing Baker was slower.*

He removed his shirt and poured water into a basin and carefully cleaned the scratch on his shoulder lest it become infected. "More damned filth and bugs in this place," he muttered as he washed the slight wound.

Frustrated and tense about being kept "prisoner" for so many weeks, Moody's temper neared boiling as he stared into the small cracked mirror. Something had to happen – and soon. One way or another they had to get out of San Felipe. There had to be a way.

Jake reluctantly joined Fuentes who was celebrating the successful showdown with more than usual gusto in the cantina. The Mexican ordered beer and tequila for all present and insisted Jake drink with him. "You see? My people like what I do," he boasted. "It gives them pleasure to see gringos shooting at each other," he said, laughing almost maniacally.

Jake only nodded. This was a side of Diego Fuentes he distinctly did not like. When Diego had held him prisoner all those months, several times Jake saw the man become drunk with pleasure and power when he executed someone who had committed what he deemed a crime against him. Diego's problem was that he became so drunk with glory he failed to see that his cruel and sadistic behavior oftentimes caused the onlookers, those he wished to impress, to grow disgusted and even more fearful of him.

Glancing around the room, Jake detected distrust and loathing on the faces of some of the cantina's patrons as they watched the big Mexican. He saw others furtively look his direction with sympathy written in their eyes. Jake knew Diego feared losing the respect and what he thought was love of his people. The man often ranted about the upstarts attempting to take control of his territory. If the looks of the Mexicans in the cantina were indicative of the people in northern Baja, Jake knew that Diego had reason to worry.

"Come, my friend, you must cheer up," Diego all but shouted as he gulped a shot of tequila. "Tell you what we'll do! Let's get us some women. It will be a night. A young girl will put a smile on your face!" He motioned to two of his men who immediately came forward. "Get us two girls," he said in a low voice. "*Young*," he emphasized. "Pretty little ones."

"Diego," Jake said, hoping Fuentes wouldn't explode in anger, "maybe that's not the best thing to do right now? The locals may not…" but Diego angrily interrupted as Jake suspected he would.

"You criticize what I do for you? You are rejecting my offer of hospitality?" Diego demanded, his words slurring slightly and eyes narrowing.

"I'm not criticizing, Diego. The people are loving you now. Perhaps they will not love you so much if you take their young daughters."

Diego's face grew red and the big man glared at Jake for several seconds. Then he picked up another shot of tequila and downed it. "Ha!" he roared. "You think of me. You think to safeguard me!" Diego exclaimed. Somehow the look in his eyes did not match the words he uttered or the tone he used. "Tell you what, my amigo, and you listen to me. I will get you a young girl and I will not take a refusal. Do you understand me?"

Both men locked eyes now. Jake could not pretend to like what Diego demanded of him. "You liked the girl I gave you when you were my guest, no? So you will like this one!" Diego said with finality.

Minutes later Diego's men dragged two young girls through the doorway and shoved them at the feet of the Mexican as they cried for mercy. Judging by the redness on their faces, they'd been slapped about. Jake glanced toward the door and saw the bloodied, furious face of a man – no doubt the girls' father. Fernando drew his weapon when he saw Jake looking at the anguished parent. "You pay him no mind," Fernando said. "If he troubles you I will shoot him. You want me to shoot?"

"Not necessary," Jake replied. He forced himself to look at the young girls sprawled on the floor. They were young – perhaps twelve or thirteen. "Well, Diego, your generosity is beyond words," he said, feigning a smile. "I'll take them both, if you don't mind. I'm sure Moody will enjoy one of them." Jake stood and pulled the girls to their feet. Neither struggled, terrified of what the big Mexican would do to them if they displeased him or the gringo.

"*Vamonos, muchachas*," Jake muttered. "Let's go, girls."

Diego, pleased that Jake had so readily bent to his demand, nodded for Fernando to accompany the three to the hotel. He then motioned for one of the cantina women to join him and he resumed drinking and loudly carousing.

Jake passed the pummeled father and tried to give him a reassuring glance. He ever-so-slightly shook his head, hoping the man could see him do so in the dim light outside the cantina.

He saw Cleary watching him from cross the street, a look of disbelief on the deputy's face.

"Maybe your young friend wants a girl?" Fernando asked.

"No. That won't be necessary," Jake answered. "I'll share." Then he called out to Cleary, "Come to my room, Daniel. We need to talk."

"You no speak Americano," Fernando complained to Jake as Cleary reluctantly fell in with the group. "You speak only my language."

Jake knocked on Moody's door as he passed. "Moody," he called through the closed door, "come to my room. Cleary will be there. We're having a little fiesta. Need you there."

Jake glanced at Fernando and repeated in Spanish what he'd just said to Moody. Fernando smiled and nodded approval.

The small room was crowded with the three men and two girls. Jake motioned for the girls to sit on the bed in case Fernando stuck his head in. The men clustered at the end of the room. "Take your shoes off in case Fernando comes in," Jake advised. "We need to look like we're serious about all this. Cleary, take your pants off."

"Why me?" Cleary demanded to know. "Make Moody take his off."

Jake and Richard glowered at the young marshal who reluctantly did as told.

"We need to look like we're cooperating," Jake explained again.

"I'll take my shirt off. Not my pants," Cleary insisted.

"Okay, we need to make a plan. Our time's up," Jake said as the girls huddled together whimpering piteously after Cleary reluctantly removed his shirt.

"Diego will force another showdown. If not tomorrow, then the next day for certain. He's grown displeased with the way things are going," Jake said. "He'd like nothing better than to return to Guerrero Negro as soon as possible."

"Displeased?" Moody commented. "Did I hear you say his majesty is 'displeased'?"

"Diego fears he's losing control of his territory, and I think he's right. I saw the looks on men's faces tonight. Not all of them like what's going on, particularly when he had the girls brought in. I think he wants to bring this little drama he's created to an end and get back to where he has more control," Jake explained.

"So, what're we going to do?" Cleary asked.

"That's what we're here to decide, kid," Jake answered.

The men fell silent for a few minutes. The only sound in the room was the quiet sobbing of the girls.

Jake moved beside the bed and squatted down. "Girls," he said in Spanish, "no harm will come to you. We won't hurt you."

"Good grief, Jake. It's come to this?" Moody muttered. "I have to say, this is the lowest point of my life – right now – here in this room."

"Well, we wouldn't be here, you ass, if you hadn't wanted to go after Baker for your own personal reasons," Cleary broke in, his voice growing louder.

"Quiet down. Now, let's make a plan," Jake urged.

They stood about, mutely looking at each other.

Minutes passed before Cleary said, "I got an idea."

"This ought to be good," Moody remarked.

Cleary cast a dirty look in Moody's direction then explained, "I've counted somewhere between eight and twelve of Diego's men around here, depending on the day. So, what if we started waylaying them, one by one, and killing them and hiding their bodies?"

"Wonderful thought, Cleary. And what do we do with our very own personal bodyguards who stalk us like shadows while we're doing all this waylaying?" Moody asked, his sarcasm unmistakable.

"So, what's your plan?" Cleary demanded. "Haven't heard any ideas from you yet."

"Simple. We start a fire in one of the buildings. There will be a lot of confusion, yelling, and general mayhem. We grab some horses while all this is going on and head south. They'll notice us missing pretty quickly but they'll no doubt expect us to head north. When we get to the next village we force someone to take us across the gulf, or we steal a boat and float away," Moody said, pleased with his idea.

"Good idea, Richard, if everything in town wasn't made of *adobe*!" Cleary scoffed. "That stuff is a bit hard to burn."

"Cleary, Moody, we have one night. This is it," Jake said, perturbed by the growing animosity between the two men. "Stop wasting time!"

"Listen," Cleary began, "my guard, Lorenzo I think his name is, sneaks off almost every night. I think he's seeing one of the girls from the cantina – after hours. Apparently he thinks I'm no threat," he paused and glared at Moody. "So, while Lorenzo or whatever in the hell he calls himself is out, I could help take out your man, Jake, then we could both take out yours, Moody. That gives us maybe four hours or so to get away."

"That would have to happen tonight," Jake said. "We don't know if Diego keeps a man in the stables or not."

"Well, there'd be three of us against one of them. What could go wrong?" Cleary asked.

"Cleary, I'll give you credit for a half good idea," Moody said. "But there are just too many things that could go wrong. If we get caught, which is highly likely, we'll be skinned and hanged, or skinned and have our toe nails torn out, or some such nonsense."

"Listen, I've heard a couple good possibilities," Jake said, trying to buoy the men's spirits. "Let's keep thinking."

Cleary slipped his shirt on while Moody drummed his fingers on the bureau. Jake paced two steps in one direction then was forced to turn and pace two steps in the other.

"We could arrange it so that if Moody is shooting at me, he misses, but I collapse as though I'm hit," Daniel suggested.

Jake shook his head no. After a moment, he said to Moody, "Hey, you and Baker each got two bullets tonight, right?"

Moody nodded.

"So, we salvaged one. That would give us five bullets the next time, assuming Diego hands out two bullets apiece." Jake stopped pacing and faced the others. "What if both gunmen fire at Diego and his men. If we could take out five of them…"

"Right. Twelve minus five leaves seven of them to riddle us with holes," Moody said.

"What if we steal some more cartridges?" Daniel asked.

"And from whom do you plan to steal them?" Moody questioned.

"Well, from Diego's men. Who else? Or maybe we could try and buy some from the locals."

"Not a bad idea, Cleary," Jake said before Moody could respond negatively. "I could approach a few tomorrow who've acted friendly when they've seen me." Jake stopped short. The idea now sounded ridiculous. Who would give the fugitives ammunition to use against the most powerful man in Baja? If caught they'd be tortured and executed. Probably their families too. "Never mind," he muttered. "Anyone helping us would be in jeopardy, along with their families."

As though reading his mind, Moody said, "Jake, that's not a totally bad idea. And you're right, we have to do something. I agree with you that Diego is wanting to bring this show to a close. Your idea of trying to get some extra help is the best one so far. You speak their language, and their kids like you. I don't know – maybe you should give it a try."

Cleary nodded in agreement.

"What about Cleary's idea of trying to overpower the guards and just stealing some horses?" Jake asked. "That pretty much worked for us once before."

"Yes, and I'm betting that Diego has those horses well-guarded because of it," Moody said.

A silence again fell on the three men. Finally Cleary asked, "So, should we vote? How do you guys handle things like this?"

"This is not a democracy, Cleary. We do what Jake decides," Moody said.

“I have no answers right now,” Jake admitted. “Let’s just be alert tomorrow. Avoid Diego if at all possible. Stay out of the cantina tomorrow night. Keep your eyes open for any stray guns laying around, I guess. That’s the best I have for right now. God help us.”

“The man did not hurt us,” Maria Santiago said to her distressed father after Jake escorted the girls to their small home the next morning.

Senor Santiago looked questioningly at his oldest daughter, a girl of thirteen. “What do you mean? The man did not hurt you?”

“None of the men hurt us,” the girl replied. “They just talked. I think they are worried. Very worried.”

Senor Santiago pulled both girls to him and hugged them tightly. He mumbled a prayer and stroked their heads, thanking the Lord for the safe delivery of his daughters. “And the man did not hurt you either, Rosa?” he asked the younger girl, his eyes brimming with tears.

“No Papa. The men just talk. The one man speaks our language, and he tried to make us less afraid,” Rosa said. “Senior Diego will not have him killed and fed to the dogs like the other gringos, will he, Papa?”

Santiago smiled. “No Rosa,” he said. “I pray not.”

“Can we help them?”

“No. I see no way,” Senor Santiago replied.

17

San Felipe bristled with tension and excitement the day following the showdown between Richard Moody and Floyd Baker. Every man who'd been present at the gunfight the night before knew that there would be another gunfight, most likely that night. Few townspeople had escaped Diego Fuentes' wrath and curses. The man had grown increasingly unreasonable and dissatisfied with everything, and his short-temper had grown even shorter, making him even more irascible. The big Mexican flew into a rage over any detail that did not please him or was not perfect. The townspeople wanted the fight over and Fuentes to leave.

The morning following the showdown, Fuentes sat, his hands supporting his aching head as he drank a cup of strong *pulque*. Several of his men stood about, hoping he did not lash out at one of them for some undetectable movement or tiny noise. Finally, he looked up with bloodshot eyes and sought out Fernando. "So, you take the girls and Jake to the hotel last night?" he asked.

"Si, Senor Fuentes."

"Well, what happened?"

"Senor Fuentes, Senor Silver had his friends join him. I think he said it was a party…a fiesta," Fernando replied, a nervous tic troubling his left eye.

Fuentes studied Fernando for several minutes before responding. For some reason, he could not see Jake Silver allowing others to debase the girls considering how objectionable the Americano had found the idea. "Hmm," Fuentes finally uttered, so hungover he was unable to think clearly or reason things out.

Fuentes slowly leaned back in his chair. Something was not right. "Get Jake Silver. Bring him here," he ordered.

By noon it had been settled. Diego decreed that Moody and Cleary would face each other that very night. The survivor would immediately face Jake Silver. "Don't think of missing, my friend. You can kill Moody. I watched him last night. He is not so fast as you. Perhaps his recent injury still plagues him. You kill him and you are free to go. If you try anything else, I will…"

Jake interrupted, "Yes. I know. I'll be skinned alive and fed to the dogs. That it, Fuentes? That all you got?"

Diego nodded toward the door, dismissing Jake without speaking.

Moody and Cleary waited at the hotel for Jake's return. His face said it all.

"Who goes first?" Moody asked.

"You and Cleary. Then me and whoever is left standing."

"Hope you don't have any more friends like Fuentes," Moody said.

"You're right, Richard. I should've let you kill him when we had the chance. It was crazy on my part to let the man live."

"What I want to know is, do we have a plan for tonight?" Cleary asked, urgency in his voice.

Both men looked at the young marshal, but neither spoke.

"Well, I have an idea," Cleary said. When no one responded, he asked, "Anyone want to hear it?"

"Sure, kid," Jake replied.

"I think the best thing to do is this. One of us, or both of us for that matter, fires at Fuentes. With two of us shooting, we're bound to hit him. Maybe a hullabaloo will happen and there'll be so much commotion that we stand a chance – if not, well, at least we took the bastard out."

"Sounds good to me," Moody said. "And remember, we're probably going to be issued two bullets. So don't waste any. We'll both take a shot at Fuentes, then take aim and shoot someone else."

"That's not a bad idea, Daniel. I'll try to make a grab for someone's weapon. If I'm lucky I'll get a shot or two off," Jake said, nodding approval.

"Okay then. We got a plan!" Cleary said, smiling. "I feel better already."

"Since it's all settled, let's get something to eat," Jake suggested.

"I'm sick and tired of the damn food here," Moody commented. "I never want to eat another stinking tamale again. I always wanted a big, juicy steak for my last meal. Thought I'd be hung – never imagined anything like this happening."

"Well, don't give up. You may get a steak and a hanging yet if tonight goes better than we all kind of think it will," Jake said, heading out the door.

Jake smiled as the three crossed the street. Moody and Cleary were clearly in good spirits. Having a plan, and having their captivity come to an end, had definitely improved their dispositions. Jake fought back a pang of sorrow, however, and tried not to think of Maggie and little Henry at home, waiting for his return. He also wondered what the real motivation was behind Fuentes' impromptu decision to have the shootout that very night. Jake couldn't help but notice that Fuentes had looked at him in a different way. The hell with him, Jake thought. The man had once been bold, audacious, even a bit dashing. Now, he seemed like a mean, sadistic monster.

During lunch Moody and Cleary decided they would return to the hotel after eating and practice how they would proceed come performance time. "We need to have a perfect routine and outcome.

Timing needs to be perfect. Positioning perfect. Plus, I have some tricks that might help us last a few minutes longer," Moody said.

"All of a few minutes?" Cleary teased.

"You never know when the posse might show up," Moody retorted, smiling.

"Well, while you two are practicing for your killer act, I'm going to see what I can do to help out. You know," Jake continued, lowering his voice, "I've noticed a lot of these Mexicans carry machetes around. If I could get my hands on one of those, I could do some damage."

"Good idea," Moody said. "You could hide it under your long coat. I'm thinking we should 'dress up' for the performance. Jake, if you could get a few of those machetes, Cleary and I could each carry one under long coats also. In fact, maybe you could put yours to use this afternoon and take out a couple of Fuentes' men. No one will suspect you if a machete is used. Diego will think the locals are getting restless, and that'll leave fewer shooting at us."

"We should have thought of the machete idea long ago," Cleary said. "You're right, Richard. Diego will think the locals are rebelling because of the way his men have been treating them."

"Well, 'better late than never' as they say," Moody replied. "But the machete idea is a damn good idea, Jake."

"The only problem is I have one of Fuentes' men following me everywhere. It's going to be tough to get anything past him," Jake said.

"Maybe he'll have to be your first victim then," Moody suggested.

Cleary piped up next. "I bet if you approached those little girls' father he'd be willing to help you out. If anybody is indebted to us, it's him. How can he say no?"

Jake hesitated. "The problem with that, Daniel, is if he gets found out, Diego will do horrible things to the girls. The father will be forced to watch, and then he'll be mutilated also. I just don't want to put him or those girls in danger."

"You might not have to. Look across the street. He's over there by the hotel. Probably waiting for you, Jake," Moody said.

"I'll see you guys later this afternoon," Jake said, getting up from the table. "Go and rehearse. I'll try and let you know from time to time what's going on."

"What time is the performance tonight?" Moody asked.

"He wanted it at sunset," Jake replied. "I suggested he'd have a more interesting evening if he held the event once it grows dark. I recommended he have torches set out for lighting – assured him it would be top entertainment and people would talk about it for years to come."

"That'll work extremely well," Moody said, happier than Jake had seen him in weeks. "It'll be harder for them to see us if we hit the dirt after we shoot," Moody explained, looking at Cleary. "If mayhem breaks out, we can last longer than just a minute or two."

"Never thought I'd look forward to a gunfight," Cleary said, "but I'm plain excited about this one."

Jake crossed the street with a Mexican following him. "Senor," Jake said, "I need to speak with Senor Santiago alone. I have to explain about the girls and what happened to them. Go have a beer. You can watch me from the cantina."

The man happily nodded and turned back to the cantina.

"Senor Santiago," Jake greeted the man. "I am most sorry about your daughters being taken by Diego's men."

"Senor Silver," Santiago began, "I come to thank you for not hurting my girls."

"We must keep that a secret," Jake said in a low voice. "Never speak of that again."

"Si, Senor, as you wish," Santiago replied, bowing slightly. "But I have prayed and the Lord has heard me. Senor Silver, it would be my honor to help you tonight. Everyone in town is talking about the upcoming gunfight. Many in the town like you and no longer like Senor Fuentes and his men who come here and abuse us," Santiago said, lowering his voice. "I have gone to Padre Alfonso and asked his forgiveness for what I am about to do." Santiago quickly made the sign of the cross. "Padre Alfonso says what I do is not a sin. For this I am thankful."

Santiago did not speak for several moments. Jake waited, but finally asked, "What are you thinking of doing?"

"I will send my daughters to you again this evening at sunset. They will have something most valuable for you. Do not turn them away until you see what they have to offer," Santiago said.

"Very well. I'll look forward to seeing them. But please do *not* put them in any danger."

"A person cannot live like a slave in his own home forever. My daughters are brave and want to do this for me, for us…but mostly for you, senor."

Jake worried about what Santiago might ask the young girls to do, but he could read the desperation and determination in the man's eyes. Santiago was right – a man could only take so much, and Diego had dished out more insults and inflicted more agony to the locals than any person had reason to tolerate.

Jake looked across the street and saw his guard engaged in lively conversation with several of Diego's men. Now would be a good time to slip out the back and look for a machete.

While Jake strolled about the town that afternoon and stole two machetes, one from the stable and another from a wagon, Moody and

Cleary made various plans for how to best take out Diego Fuentes. Both were in a jovial mood knowing their situation would soon come to an end, one way or the other.

Near sunset Roberto knocked on Jake's door. "Senor Silver, your little friends have returned. Perhaps they are eager for more?" Roberto asked, a lewd grin on his face when Jake opened the door.

Looking down, Jake saw the two Santiago girls, both so beautiful and fragile, standing before him. Neither looked him in the eye, but instead nervously stared at the floor. Rosa clung to her sister's hand and finally peeked at Jake and smiled shyly.

Jake stood aside so the girls could enter and then he closed the door. Putting his finger to his lips, he motioned for them to follow him to the far corner of the room. "We must speak very softly," he said. "Whisper."

Maria Santiago nodded in understanding. Letting go of Rosa's hand, she carefully removed the shawl draped over her head and shoulders. A leather bag secured inside the shawl held two dozen cartridges that she offered to Jake.

Jake smiled at the offer. "Well, if I had a gun to fit these, this gift would be most welcome," he said. "Thank you for your thought, though."

Then Rosa turned around and Maria unfastened her sister's dress. Strapped to Rosa's back was an old, large handgun. "Padre Alfonso's gun," the girl whispered. "It is blessed, too," she said, her eyes shining.

"I'm sure it is," Jake said, smiling broadly. "*Muchas gracias, muchachas*," he said. "Many thanks, girls."

That night Diego Fuentes allotted Cleary and Moody two cartridges each. "You know my rules," Diego said. "Need I repeat them?" When neither man answered he continued. "Now, the man left standing will face Jake Silver. If the survivor of this round is too wounded to continue, I have a new rule. Jake Silver will face two of my best gunmen. That is only fair, no? Since he is so quick to 'clear leather'… as you Americanos say."

"I'd like to use my own gun, Senor Fuentes," Cleary said. "If I have to face Silver and Moody, I should have my own weapon."

"Very strong thinking," Diego commented. He thought about Cleary's request for a few moments, then said to Jorge, "Give these men their own weapons. Perhaps Mr. Moody will be faster then, yes?"

It took several minutes for Cleary's and Moody's weapons to be produced, and the crowd grew more excitable while waiting. Moody looked about for Jake and finally spied him standing among Fuentes' men. "Wonder where the hell he's been all afternoon." Moody said in a low voice.

"He's probably been searching for…things," Cleary responded. "And by the look on his face I'd say he met with some success. At least I sure as hell hope so. I'm getting a bit tense."

"Relax, Daniel. This'll all be over in a few minutes – one way or the other. Think of this as a grand performance, not a desperate idea."

Both men fell silent as Diego moved toward them with their weapons.

"Now, the rule is, I will drop my arm when it is time for you to draw your weapons. You cannot shoot before that time," Diego said. "It is all just like last night. Surely you remember the rules?" he repeated.

"Kind of hard to see your arm in the dark, Senor Fuentes," Cleary said. "Maybe you could stand by that torch over there. We could see you better. People could watch you then, too."

"Yes, I will do so," Diego said, looking around. "That is a most excellent idea."

"Clever boy," Moody said as Diego moved toward a torch. "Make sure you don't hit Jake, and take a last look where Diego's men are stationed."

"I've got their locations memorized," Cleary said. "I'll take someone on Diego's right side. You go for his left. There's more men there and you have an extra bullet."

"Now you're giving orders?" Moody laughed. "Just don't hit Jake."

The crowd grew quiet as Diego took his place and dramatically raised his right arm above his head. He held his arm aloft for a full ten seconds again, letting the tension build. Just as suddenly as it came down, Moody's and Cleary's guns exploded. Both men immediately dropped to the ground and rolled away from each other. As Moody hoped, pandemonium set in after the first shots. When both men dropped, most of the onlookers thought the gunmen had shot each other. Almost instantly, however, more shots were fired, and three of Diego's men dropped. These blasts were quickly followed by several more shots that hit men in the crowd. Panic struck as people were unable to tell who was doing all the firing. Then someone knocked over a torch, plunging everyone into darkness, and the panicked crowd exploded in pandemonium.

Suddenly a voice cried out, "Diego! Diego Fuentes has been shot!" More gunshots sounded among the onlookers. People scattered as bullets flew in all directions and chaos reigned.

Moody and Cleary remained motionless on the ground, hoping their adversaries would think them dead. To get up and run at this moment invited death.

Moody could tell by the ruckus and shouting that mayhem now prevailed. He heard the dull thud of clubs smashing skulls and smelled the blood of people being hacked by machetes. The melee last but a few minutes, but they seemed like the longest minutes he'd ever lived through. Then he heard people running pell-mell swearing and yelling. Someone stepped on his hand and another tripped over him. In the distance women screamed and men cursed.

Suddenly Jake knelt by his side. "You alive in there, Moody?"

"No, I'm not. But don't tell anyone."

"Good, Cleary's alive but wounded. Not bad, though."

Moody dared to open one eye and saw Jake reloading an old revolver. "Where'd you get that monster, amigo?"

"You wouldn't believe me if I told you," Jake said, snapping the revolver closed.

"Tell me anyway. I'm just laying around with nothing to do."

"Santiago's girls paid me a visit this afternoon. The gun and ammunition are compliments of Father Alfonso. They've even been blessed," Jake said, grinning. "Listen, Diego's men are scattering and the locals have gone crazy chasing after them. I kind of think those bandits wore out their welcome in San Felipe. I doubt anyone will attack us now, but with mobs you never know, so get to the stables. There's three horses in there, compliments of Fuentes. I picked out his best. Get Cleary and the two of you take off and head south. I'll follow in a bit."

"No. We all leave together or nothing," Moody said, sitting up and brushing off his suit coat. "Hey, by the way, good idea to have us wear these tonight. I'm sure it made it harder to see us here in the dark. Good thinking."

"Moody, I'm not here to chat. Now get the hell out of here!" Jake yelled, standing and watching figures fleeing in the dark. "Get Cleary and get out while you can!"

Moody stood quickly and faced Jake, only inches from him. "You know what, Silver? I'm damn sick and tired of you issuing orders. You think because you wear a tin badge that you're the boss. I have news for you. I'm not going until you're with us. I have no intention of coming all the way back down here again to save your sorry ass. So shut the hell up and help me with Cleary. This is over, you hear me? It's time to make tracks, as *you're* so fond of saying."

Reluctantly Jake shoved the heavy weapon under his belt. "I'd sure as hell like to get my own guns back. I wonder where Diego put them."

"Jake, new ones are on me. Let's go," Moody said as he helped Cleary to his feet. "You hurt bad?" he asked the young man.

"No. Just stings like holy hell," Cleary said.

"Okay. Now you'll have a scar you can be proud of. Women love scars, by the way. It'll drive your little Josephine wild. Can you ride?" Moody asked, noticing Cleary's limp.

"I could run if I had to," Cleary answered.

The three men quickly moved to the stable, mounted up and headed south out of San Felipe. "Aren't we going the wrong way?" Moody shouted.

"No. I doubt anyone will look for us in this direction. I'll explain later," Jake answered. "Just put the spurs to those horses and ride."

The men traveled as quickly as they could through the saguaro and other cacti before Jake finally slowed their procession, everyone sweaty from the difficult travel through the rugged terrain.

"How far we going?" Cleary asked, his face pinched with pain.

"We're going until the horses drop or until we get to Puertocitos," Jake replied. "You sure you're okay, Cleary?"

He watched the young man nod, then said, "Listen, we have to make it to Puertocitos. It's a small fishing village well south of San Felipe. If we take the road, we run the chance of coming across bandits, or maybe even Fuentes' fleeing men. Our only good chance is to ride cross-country. It's going to be very tough going. It'll be fewer miles than taking the road, but unfortunately it won't be faster, only safer – at least until someone figures out what we've done."

They slowed the horses to a walk and no one spoke for a long spell. Finally, Moody asked, "So what do we do in Puertocitos? Go fishing? Open a cantina?"

Jake looked at his friend. “No, Richard, I’m going to take you on a boat ride again.”

It was several moments before Moody responded. “I’m speechless. I don’t have words to express myself or what I think about this.”

“What? No fancy quote from Shakespeare, or Virgil?”

“I never thought the day would come when you wouldn’t have something to say, Richard,” Cleary said.

“You think this is funny, kid? We’ll see how you feel when we get there,” Moody said, shaking his head. “Just tell me, Jake, that you prearranged all this. Even if it’s a lie, just tell me that.”

“Sure, Richard, whatever you say.”

18

Although traveling much more slowly than expected, the three men arrived in Puertocitos having had no encounters with bandits or trouble from Fuentes' surviving men. With dry, cracked lips and a parched mouth, Jake negotiated a jug of water from the occupants of the first small hut they came to.

"Where'd you learn to talk their language?" Cleary asked after guzzling a half the jug of water.

"I grew up on a ranch in Texas. A lot of Mexicans worked for my father," Jake explained. "Not so fast on the water intake. You'll get sick."

"You ever wish you were a rancher and not a lawman?" Cleary asked, wiping his mouth. "Especially when you're in situations like this?"

"I did once. That time passed, though," Jake answered, a solemn look on his face as he remembered his plans to retire from the law, marry Betsy, and become a rancher.

The town of Puertocitos did not really exist as a town. Several dozen small huts with adjoining palapas sat scattered along the beach. Fishing nets and small boats were strewn carelessly about the area which reeked of rotting fish carcasses.

"I was feeling hungry until I smelled this stuff," Cleary said, his face pale with shadows under his eyes.

"We'll get some food and more water, and then we'll make a plan," Jake said, assessing Cleary's condition. "We can stay a few days and rest up if needed. I don't think we'll be troubled here."

Moody was uncharacteristically silent, but Jake could tell by the man's face that he wasn't happy with their situation.

"We'll talk later," Jake said, looking directly at Moody. "Meanwhile, I'll arrange for a boat and some supplies. Let's head over there where the beach is clean of garbage and set ourselves up," Jake suggested, pointing to an area with relatively clean sand, a palapa for shade, and some palm stumps to sit on.

Within an hour the men had eaten their fill of fish tortillas and mostly quenched their thirst while an older woman tended to Cleary's red, angry-looking thigh wound. "Didn't know a bullet graze could hurt this bad," he mumbled.

"Stay in the law business and you might find out what one feels embedded in your body," Moody commented.

"Okay. Everyone feeling better now?" Jake asked, trying to sound jovial. "You guys get some rest. I'll arrange for a boat and captain."

Moody shook his head in exasperation. "Sure thing, Jake. And you think I'm going to sail across this gulf in one of *those*?" he asked, pointing at the small, rickety-looking vessels. "Not on your life."

"What's your plan, Richard?"

"I can damn well ride out of here."

"You think so?"

"I know full well I can. You and I have done it before."

Jake squatted down, eye-level with Moody. "You can try, but you won't make it. The little Mexican over there already told me that Fuentes' men were here yesterday looking for us – *tres gringos* – three gringos. Some of Fuentes' surviving men apparently regrouped and took the road south so they missed us, but they'll not quit looking until they find us, Richard. They'll want revenge. We have maybe a total of four bullets left. That's it."

"No. Don't tell me. Silver, remind me to shoot you when we get back," Moody said, sighing heavily and looking away. "If you planned a sea journey for an escape, you could have had the decency to hire the captain of the *Sea Goddess.* At least that boat didn't look like it was going to sink in an hour."

"Quit your belly-aching, Moody. The trip will only take a day or two at most. I asked a fisherman in San Felipe while we were there," Jake said, knowing he stretched the truth.

Moody abruptly stood and stalked away.

Cleary asked, "He gonna come with us?"

"Probably." Jake looked closely at the young marshal. "How you doing, Daniel?"

"Better now that I've eaten. But I'm going with you, Jake. I don't think I could ride very far right now. My leg is really throbbing."

Jake nodded. "I'll go and get us a boat – and hopefully someone who'll take us across."

None of the locals would help the men. They'd been warned, and their families threatened. Only Juan Carlos was brave enough to even talk to them.

"They be back soon, senor," Juan said. "You must go. Go now. If they find you here, they will kill us, all of us, for giving you food and water."

"I need a boat, Juan. A good boat."

"No boat, senor."

"I have three horses, Juan. They're yours if you get me a boat."

Jake could see Juan considering the offer. "Senor, I take the horses. You must steal the boat in exchange. We cannot give one to you."

"Juan, how will they know I stole it and that you didn't give it to me?" Jake asked, growing exasperated.

"You must hit me many times. Then I look like I am robbed," Juan explained.

"Juan," Jake said, "I cannot beat you. I won't hit you." Jake looked at the Mexican, probably a mestizo judging by his small size.

"I find someone to hit me for you," Juan said, his face brightening. "I take the horses. You then steal the boat. I go get hit. You leave now."

Unable to secure a better deal for the small man, Jake resigned himself to the fact that Juan was willing to face a beating to get the three horses. The little Mexican picked out a boat and the two of them pushed it into the water so Jake could be assured that there were no leaks. Juan then showed Jake a sail – at least that's what Jake thought it was. The weathered, frayed hank of cloth had definitely seen better days. There were also paddle-like oars in the craft. Last, the Mexican loaded the boat with water and as many provisions as he and a few of his neighbors could afford to give away.

"You leave now. Good time. Chubasco come tonight so you have good wind to travel," Juan said.

Jake had no idea what a chubasco was, but he nodded his appreciation.

"We leave this afternoon," he announced to Cleary and Moody when he returned to their area. "I found us a sound boat," he said, again trying to buoy the men's spirits. "It's got sails and oars, food and water. Almost as nice as the *Sea Goddess,* Moody." His effort at humor failed, and he stood, studying the solemn faces. "You coming with us, Moody?"

"I suppose."

For the first two hours of the journey Jake rowed. He hummed as he did so, trying to make light of the almost impossible journey before them. He remembered all too well the horrific pounding he'd taken from the monstrous seas and wind on a much larger vessel that he'd traveled on from Puerto Penasco a month or so ago, but he felt they had no other viable option. Not even sure of the exact direction to head, he simply rowed northeasterly, figuring that land would appear eventually, then they could travel up the coast to Puerto Penasco.

Puertocitos slowly faded from view as it grew dark, and all three of the travelers began to feel a sense of relief that they might actually be free of Fuentes' men. None of them had talked much that afternoon, everyone lost in his own worries and thoughts. Daniel had slept most of the time, and Jake worried that the boy might grow feverish, not a good sign.

"How much food do you think we have?" Moody finally asked, looking through various small baskets and containers.

"Probably enough to make landfall if we eat sparingly," Jake said. "Those people hardly had enough for themselves. I felt bad taking what little they had."

"I'm sure all that horse flesh will be mighty tasty to them," Moody suggested.

"You want to row for a spell?" Jake asked.

"No," Moody replied matter-of-factly. "I'm thinking we should put up that sail, if that's what that dirty piece of canvas is. The air feels a bit strange, like maybe we could get some weather. But not being the seagoing expert that you are.... Anyway, we might be able to make more distance if we have a sail up also as we row."

Jake stopped rowing and looked around the boat. "Hell! We have no mast to hang that thing on."

"I think this is supposed to be a mast...sort of," Moody said, picking up a long, wooden pole.

"That big stick?"

"Yep."

The two men fiddled around with the gear for more than an hour, trying to figure out how the sail could be raised. They didn't notice the wind rising until a large gust hit them.

Moody looked at the darkening sky. "Oh damn! I think I know what a chubasco is."

"Yeah. I'm getting a good idea myself."

The wind gusted to sixty that night, and it was all Jake and Richard could do to keep the boat from capsizing. Several times the little craft was stood on end, and twice it rolled so far abeam that water ran over the gunnels swamping them. They bailed like madmen to stay afloat. Swells rapidly formed and white caps stretched across the horizon. Jake tried to console himself as he and Richard struggled to keep the boat afloat that at least they were being pushed in the right direction. For several hours the chubasco raged until finally the storm blew itself out and the seas slowly began to lay down. Exhausted, both men fell asleep, adrift in the vast, silent gulf.

The sun was up when the Jake opened his eyes and saw Richard Moody rowing. Neither spoke as he rummaged in the baskets trying to salvage what rain-soaked food he could. After a bit he asked, "Has Cleary been awake yet?"

"Yeah. He was rowing when I woke up," Moody said.

"How's he looking?"

"Looked okay. A bit tired and weak, but I think he'll be okay."

The breakfast of soggy tortillas at least filled them up and the three tried to con themselves into feeling better.

"The way I see it," Jake said as he passed a water jug around, "last night was probably the worst weather we'll have, and we survived. So, I have no doubt we'll make it to land."

"Ever the optimist," Moody said.

"I think we need a schedule," Cleary finally said. "We need to take turns rowing. Like maybe two hours each. Rotate. We'll at least be making progress, especially if we can keep this up day and night."

"How you feeling, kid?" Jake asked.

"Better. I can do this, Jake."

"Okay. Captain Cleary has a plan. Let's do it. If we have to stop at night and drift, then so be it, I guess."

"I don't think we can afford to do that, Jake. We could drift off course, or backwards for that matter. I think Daniel's right. We row day and night. We should make land in a few days at most if we can keep at it," Moody said.

Jake nodded his approval. "Okay, I'll take the first stretch. Hey, Daniel, there's some fishing gear of some sort under that seat there that Juan left for us. Why don't you do some fishing while we're out here? Maybe that'll help with the food supply. To be honest, most of what we had was ruined last night."

**

One day passed. Two days. Three days. No land appeared. No one talked about their predicament. Fortunately, they caught a steady supply of fish which they ate raw, so starvation was not imminent, although the drinking water was running low. They filled their hours with needling Daniel about his "girlfriend" and reliving the events of their recent time in Baja.

"Jake, you really should have seen Casanova here when he laid eyes on Josephine," Moody teased. "I thought it was going to be Romeo and Juliet all over."

"I don't know who Casanova or those other people are," Cleary retorted, "but you are exaggerating."

Moody only looked at the young man and arched an eyebrow.

"Now listen here, Moody, just because I showed a bit of courtesy and concern, is no reason for your wild talk."

Jake thoroughly enjoyed the banter between the two and laughed aloud.

"So, tell me about her," Jake finally said. "I've not had the pleasure of meeting your lady."

"She's not my lady, Jake. She's just a real pretty, beautiful actually, young girl who got kidnapped. She…" Daniel stopped, as though becoming aware that he had said too much already.

It was Daniel who finally figured out how to put the sail onto the "stick," which gave them all a little lift. From then on they rowed and sailed, although often the afternoon winds became so strong they had to lower the sail.

Ten days after leaving Puertocitos, Jake swore he saw land. "I'm mighty glad to hear that," Cleary said. "We just lost the last bit of fishing line."

"Aren't you supposed to say 'Land Ahoy'?" Moody asked.

"Land Ahoy!" Jake shouted, pointing and grinning.

Each man put more into his rowing strokes after that announcement. While one rowed, the other two kept their eyes plastered in the direction where Jake had seen land.

"I see it now!" Cleary shouted after an hour of eye strain. "I see it!"

With land definitely in sight, the mood in the small vessel abruptly changed to excitement.

"Do they have restaurants in that town?" Cleary asked. "I want some real food. I never want to eat fish again as long as I live."

"I don't remember," Jake said. "But probably."

"I want a bath and a shave," Moody said. "Then I want a bottle of whiskey and a steak. A big, big steak. And you're buying, Marshal Silver."

Although land had been visible, after a few hours the men felt they'd made no headway because of the northerly brisk wind. Disappointment about not making landfall stole their earlier joviality, and Cleary worried that they might miss land altogether if the wind or current took them in the wrong direction when it turned dark. Moody grew taciturn.

"Tell you what," Jake said after a bit, "we're going to have a minor change of plans. We'll now have one person on lookout, one person rowing, and one person bailing. Looks like we've sprung a leak."

So the night went, but just before dawn all three smelled the sweet aroma of land, and shortly after they heard the sound of a small surf hitting the beach. "Hell I can swim that far if I have to," Jake commented.

Within an hour the boat's keel dragged on sand, bringing the sinking craft to a stop.

Sunburned, seasick, and stinking like hell, the raggedy trio wobbled and staggered as they disembarked from the rickety vessel and tried to walk on land. "Damn! I could kiss the ground I'm so happy to be alive and off that boat," Cleary commented. "And you guys stink something awful!"

"Longest days of my life, Silver," Moody said.

"Hey, you're here and alive. Quit complaining. I agree the trip took a bit longer than I thought it would, but we'd still be on the trail if we'd headed for Ensenada and then north to Tijuana, so think about that."

"Cleary, hang out with Jake Silver here and you'll have lots of episodes almost as fun as this little journey across the gulf," Moody said as the three slowly stumbled up the beach "This one might be hard to out-do, though."

"How we gonna get back to Arizona?" Cleary asked.

"Simple, boys." Jake pulled a leather money pouch from his vest.

"Where'd you come up with that?" Moody asked.

"Well, I'm ashamed to admit it, but when Diego went down, I couldn't see letting all that money fall into the wrong hands. I figured he owed us after all the hell he put us through, not to mention our horses and gear he confiscated. I think there's plenty here to buy three horses and some tack," Jake said, grinning. "Dinner and drinks too."

"Hear that, Cleary? You're traveling with a thief. A regular pickpocket," Moody said.

"Looks like I'll have to arrest you both," Cleary commented, "when we get back, of course."

Horses took several days for Jake to procure, but neither Moody nor Cleary complained. Happy to be on land again, well fed, clean, and free of Diego Fuentes and his army of cutthroats, the two wiled away their afternoons drinking beer and sitting in the shade watching Jake haggle with local vendors selling branded horses that had obviously been stolen from across the border.

Finally Jake found three good animals without brands. "You know, Richard, I'm damn sure this is the horse that Thomas Jefferson loaned you that you left in Yuma," Jake said, as he saddled the animal. "I'll just return him to my ranch hand if you don't mind."

19

Three days later the men reached the border. That night, camped on the Arizona side, Moody announced he wouldn't be heading back to Prescott with Jake and Cleary.

"I'm going to San Diego, Jake. Gotta find my nephew. See if he ever showed up."

"Richard, I received a letter before I left for Mexico. It's how I knew where you were. I'm sorry. I meant to give it to you when I arrived, but I completely forgot about it what with all the hoopla when you two showed up. Unfortunately, the letter is probably unreadable now," Jake said, pulling out a soggy piece of paper. "I got a little distracted, and it pretty much got soaked," Jake said.

"Well, what did he say?" Moody asked, leaning forward.

"Buddy's alive and in San Diego. He's fishing with a man named Axel Anderson, I think the name was. Something like that, anyway. The boat is the *Fisher Queen*. I remember that. I'm sure the man at the bank can tell you all that information," Jake said. "But, basically he said he doesn't want to return to Prescott. Said he wants to be a fisherman."

Moody remained silent for a bit. "Well, at least I found him. It sounds like he knows what he wants to do."

"Yeah. But he's young. Still...." Jake started to comment that the boy was too young to make those decisions but stopped. Hadn't he himself run away to be a cattle drover when he was only fourteen or fifteen? Cleary too had run-off when he was but a kid and found work on a ranch.

"I still have to see him," Moody said. "I need to make certain that he's okay and that things are as he says. If what he says is true then, well, I guess I'll have to go along with it. My sister sure wouldn't like it, but I'd be a lousy guardian, and you, sir, have your hands full. Besides, I might stay in San Diego for a spell. I like it there."

"He can always come and stay with us. You know that. It's a big house. I could use you in Prescott."

"I hear you saying that, Jake, but I saw you in Mexico. You left your daughter and nephew to basically go on an adventure," Moody said. "Don't deny it. A letter from a kid motivated you to leave hearth and home and take off. You knew you were facing almost certain death returning to Diego Fuentes' country, yet you came anyway. You didn't even know where I'd be!"

When Jake tried to argue, Moody continued. "You don't like your desk job. You're bored. I'll be surprised if you stick it out much longer, in fact. You don't need another kid under your roof."

"I'll be there until Maggie's grown up," Jake protested.

Both Cleary and Moody looked at him, and Jake saw doubt in their eyes.

The following day Moody caught the westbound train for San Diego at the Gila Bend junction.

"Will he be back?" Cleary asked as the train pulled away.

"Hard to say. I think so, though. Might be a spell."

"Jake, I need to talk about McGraw," Cleary said as the two turned to ride on.

"You don't need to explain, Daniel. You did what you had to do."

"No. I need to get this off my chest," Daniel said. "I know you wanted to be the one to kill him. To get your revenge. I respect that. But I had no choice. It was either him or Moody and me. I don't want you to hold my killing him against me. I hope you can understand."

"Yes, I do. I just – I just wanted to be the one to put him in the ground after what he did to Betsy…and me and Maggie. I shouldn't have waited. I'm really not sure why I did. I kept telling myself I'd do it once Maggie was grown and didn't need me anymore. But I'm not sure. Maybe I was kidding myself. I don't know what held me back from hunting him down like the cur he was."

"He was a big man and a good shot. But something about the man was not right. He…he – well, I don't know how to explain it. He might've killed you – not that you're not a great shot yourself, but you have reasons to live. He had none except revenge. And I think when a man has reasons to live, he might be more cautious, and that could've been your undoing. But maybe I don't know what I'm talking about."

Jake was silent for a few moments before he spoke. "He did kill me, Daniel. When he fired that rifle and killed Betsy, part of me died too. That man took the soul out of me. And Richard, as cussed and no good as he is, is the only one who can lead me back to finding it. Anyway, I didn't know how much I loved Betsy until it was too late. Don't let that happen to you. If you truly like this young girl, don't ignore her or put her off."

Cleary paused, "I suppose Richard told you all about Josephine."

Jake smiled at him. "So, you're sweet on her, huh?"

"Hell, Jake, I've only seen her once. Besides, she's too young and way too pretty to be happy with someone like me. I bet she's got lots of beaus. I don't know why Moody's heckling me so much about her."

"Well, you have to know Richard to appreciate it."

"You know, I mostly dislike that man, but every time we were in a tough spot, I was happy as hell that he was there with me," Cleary said. "I didn't know it at the time. It was always later when I was thinking about it that I realized that." Cleary rode in silence for a bit before he continued. "To be honest, he taught me a lot, but I'd never tell him that. Can't say exactly what he taught me, but it seemed to be about life – and about being a man. It all just sort of sneaked into my head. He isn't like any teacher I've ever had, I'll tell you that much. Somehow – well, I don't know how – but somehow I learned a lot from him. He could be a real bastard, though."

Jake smiled. He had no doubt that Moody had taught Cleary plenty. He could see the change in the young man.

"So, you going to stay on as Deputy U.S. Marshal?" Jake asked as the two headed for Phoenix.

"I'm thinking I will – if you'll have me," Cleary said. "I think I'm ready for the job now."

"I think you are too, Daniel."

Two weeks after the men returned to Prescott, Daniel Cleary took a jaunt down to Minnehaha Flats. He didn't know where Josephine lived, or even what her last name was, so he started his search at the small store. A bundle of nerves, he entered and immediately saw her standing behind the counter talking with a customer. He watched her for a full minute before she looked his way: her face so animated; her laugh like music. He liked how her eyes sparkled when she smiled. He felt his face grow warm just watching her.

"My! Marshal Cleary. It's been a spell since you've been in," Josephine said, blushing and smoothing first her hair, then her dress, when she saw him.

"You look mighty nice today, Josephine," Cleary said, shifting from foot to foot.

"Oh, I'm…I'm…." The girl looked about helplessly. Finally, she gained some composure, "What can I help you with, Marshal?"

"I came to see you, Josephine. I been thinking about you quite a bit since I was here last. I couldn't come back right away because I was chasing those two bad men who caused you all that trouble and, and uh, I went all the way to Mexico to find them."

"Yes, I heard that you and the other man were gone."

"Who'd you hear that from?" Cleary asked.

"Oh…oh…," she stammered, "well, I had to go to Prescott once for supplies and I just happened to stop by the sheriff's office, and he mentioned about you and Marshal Silver and Mr. Moody being gone…and all. It sounded so…so exciting…and scary."

Cleary nodded and fiddled with his hat. "Wish I'd been there in Prescott to see you," he said after a moment. "I would've bought you some pie and coffee – if you'd a'wanted some. I wouldn't have forced you to go eat pie, of course," he said, his face growing hot at the stupidity of the statement. "Only if you wanted to."

"Oh my. Yes, I do love a good dessert. I would have enjoyed that very much." After a moment Josephine added, "Ma just made pie early this morning. Maybe you'd like to come by our house and enjoy a slice before you head back to Prescott. Oh, I do hope you're not leaving right away, though," she blurted.

"Josephine, I'll be honest and just come right out and say what I came to say. I came here to see you, and I'm wanting to ask if you'd like me to come back again to see you," Cleary said, locking eyes with the young woman. "If you have another beau you only need tell me and I'll make myself scarce."

"Why, why yes, Marshal," the girl stammered. "That would be nice. I would like very much for you to come back and visit."

"You can call me by my name. It's Daniel."

Josephine smiled. "Daniel, I would like for you to come back. I truly would. I…I confess I've thought about you often…almost every day, I guess," she said, blushing deeply. "Truthfully, I thought of you every single day and prayed for your safety."

"I need to tell you right off, and I'm probably being a bit premature, but I aim to stay a Deputy U.S. Marshal, Josephine. If you don't like that idea, you best say so now and I won't waste your time or mine."

"Being a marshal sounds wonderful. You're so brave!" Josephine said, again turning pink. "I have no objection to that. None at all."

Daniel slowly reached out for her hand. It felt so delicate and small as he wrapped his calloused hand around it. "Well, I'm pleased to know you, Josephine."

Watch for Jere D. James'
next great western in late 2016

CPSIA information can be obtained at www.ICGtesting.com
Printed in the USA
LVOW11s1914180516

488875LV00001B/76/P